Book Ten

EPIC ZERO 10

Tales of a Seriously Sore Loser

By

R.L. Ullman

But That's Another Story... Press

Epic Zero 10: Tales of a Seriously Sore Loser

Cover design and character illustrations by Yusup Mediyan.

Published by But That's Another Story… Press
Ridgefield, CT

Printed in the United States of America.
First Printing, 2022.
ISBN: 978-1-953713-67-4
Library of Congress Control Number: 2022921398

For George,
one of my childhood heroes

BOOKS BY R.L. ULLMAN

EPIC ZERO SERIES

Epic Zero: Tales of a Not-So-Super 6th Grader
Epic Zero Extra (free at rlullman.com)
Epic Zero 2: Tales of a Pathetic Power Failure
Epic Zero 3: Tales of a Super Lame Last Hope
Epic Zero 4: Tales of a Total Waste of Time
Epic Zero 5: Tales of an Unlikely Kid Outlaw
Epic Zero 6: Tales of a Major Meta Disaster
Epic Zero 7: Tales of a Long Lost Leader
Epic Zero 8: Tales of a Colossal Boy Blunder
Epic Zero 9: Tales of a Souled-Out Superhero
Epic Zero 10: Tales of a Seriously Sore Loser
Epic Zero 11: Tales of a Mere Meta Mortal
Epic Zero 12: Tales of a Cosmic Catastrophe
Epic Zero: The Epic Character Guide (at rlullman.com)

MONSTER PROBLEMS SERIES

Monster Problems: Vampire Misfire
Monster Problems 2: Down for the Count
Monster Problems 3: Prince of Dorkness

UNLEGENDARY DRAGON SERIES

Unlegendary Dragon: The Magical Kids of Lore
Unlegendary Dragon 2: The Fall of Camelot
Unlegendary Dragon 3: The Battle for Avalon

TABLE OF CONTENTS

ONE

I GET THE GIFT OF A LIFETIME

I've been kidnapped by my own parents.

"Can I take the blindfold off now?" I ask.

"No, not yet, Elliott," Dad says.

"We'll let you know when it's time," Mom adds. "Don't you trust us?"

Well, yes… and no. I mean, of course, I trust them. After all, they're not only my parents, but they're also two of the greatest superheroes in the entire universe. But I have no idea where they're taking me or why they're making me wear this blindfold.

Who knows? Maybe Grace finally convinced them to abandon me on some remote island.

"This way," Mom says as she takes my hand and

leads me off of the Freedom Flyer. "Watch your step."

"Watch my step?" I say. "Um, I can't watch anything right now. I'm blindfolded, remember?"

Mom laughs.

I wish I knew what was going on. I mean, just a few minutes ago I was eating breakfast on the Waystation when my parents showed up saying they had a surprise for me. Then, they handed me a blindfold and told me to put it on. And now, well, I don't know where we are.

Oh, no! I left my half-eaten breakfast on the table! Well, I certainly can't be held responsible for whatever mess Dog-Gone leaves behind.

"Only a few more steps," Mom says as she leads me over some unsteady ground.

This had better be good. Truthfully, I'm still run-down from rescuing Selfie in the Underworld. Facing the Orb of Oblivion—again—plus playing tug-of-war with Terrog over control of my Meta energy wiped me out. If it wasn't for Selfie, I'd probably still be down there. But luckily she hypnotized Tormentus into sending us home.

"Okay, we're here," Mom says finally.

"Now can I take this thing off?" I ask.

"Epic?" comes Selfie's voice.

"Selfie?" I say, totally confused. "Is that you?"

"Yeah," she says. "It's me. In fact, we're all here."

"All of you?" I ask. "As in, the whole team?"

"Yep," Night Owl says. "The other members of the Freedom Force blindfolded us and brought us here."

Huh? I thought it was strange that my parents blindfolded and kidnapped me, but the whole team? What are they up to?

"I'm here too," Pinball says. "And can you smell who else is here?"

"Shut it, pin-head," Skunk Girl says. "It sounds like we're all here, so can we take these blindfolds off now?"

"Yes," Dad says. "You can remove your blindfolds."

"Awesome!" Pinball exclaims. "I love surprises!"

I don't know what I was expecting, but when I take off my blindfold, this definitely wasn't it. We're standing in front of an old, Art Deco style movie theater with green bricks, boarded-up windows, and a busted marquee that's hanging precariously over the front entrance. There's a red, neon sign perched on top of the roof that reads: '-potlight Theater' because the 'S' has fallen off.

Of course, I recognize the place right away. The Spotlight Theater was Keystone City's grand movie palace back in the day. But now… well, now it's basically an abandoned cockroach motel on the outskirts of town.

I glance at my friends who look just as confused. Don't get me wrong, I love going to the movies, but I'm pretty sure no one has seen a film here in a really long time. Like, for decades.

"Oooh!" Pinball exclaims, rubbing his palms together. "Are we seeing a double feature? Extra-large popcorn, here I come!"

"We're not seeing anything in that dump," Skunk

Girl says. "And Pinball, can't you stop thinking about your stomach for, like, a second?"

"So, does that mean we're not getting popcorn?" he asks with a sad face as he rubs his belly.

"Sorry but I'm a little lost here," I say, turning to my parents. "You said you had a big surprise. Is this it?"

"Yep," Dad says with a smile as he plops his big hand on my shoulder. "Don't you like it?"

"Um, to be honest, I'm still not sure what's going on here," I say.

"Oh, stop torturing them, Captain Justice," Mom says. "TechnocRat, why don't you show them the real surprise?"

The real surprise?

"With pleasure, Ms. Understood," TechnocRat says. Then, he ignites his jetpack and hovers in front of the theater's double doors. "Okay, kiddos, this might look like an old movie theater, but trust me, it's not."

"It's not?" Selfie says confused.

"I don't want to offend him," Skunk Girl whispers to me, "but I think the rat needs some new glasses."

"Master Mime, could you give me a hand?" TechnocRat asks.

The mute hero nods and waves his hand dramatically. Just then, a giant, purple hand materializes out of thin air and sets an object on the ground in front of us. It kind of looks like a metal water bottle, except the top is glowing with a bright, blue light.

"What is that?" Night Owl asks.

"This," TechnocRat says proudly, "is a Distorter."

A Distorter? Why does that sound so familiar?

"What does it do?" Night Owl asks.

"Exactly what its name implies," TechnocRat says. "It uses holographic technology to 'distort' the appearance of objects, disguising their true form."

Disguising their true form? That's right! When I traveled to a mirror universe, Captain Justice 2 used a Distorter to make people think the Prop House was falling over. So, if TechnocRat is using a Distorter on this theater, there must be more here than meets the eye.

"So, are you saying this movie theater doesn't really look like… this?" Selfie asks.

"Not exactly," TechnocRat says, twirling his little whiskers. "I'm saying that this movie theater actually isn't a movie theater at all. Observe." Then, he cuts the jets on his jetpack and lands directly on top of the Distorter with a CLICK, turning off the blue light.

The Spotlight starts shimmering, and suddenly the decrepit theater is replaced by a shiny, modern-looking building! It's five stories tall with a silver exterior and large, black windows. I can't be certain, but it looks like it's made of pure tungsten steel!

"Whoa!" Pinball exclaims as he cranes his neck back to take it all in. "What is this place?"

"This," Dad says, "is your new secret headquarters."

"Wait, what?!" I say.

"You're kidding, right?" Night Owl asks.

"Nope," Mom says. "Say goodbye to your treehouse and hello to Next Gen's new base of operations."

"Are you serious?" I ask in total disbelief. "This is a dream, right? Someone pinch me. Ow!"

"You asked for it," Skunk Girl says with a smirk.

"This… this is incredible," Selfie says. "But why did you do this for us?"

"Because every legitimate superhero team needs a real headquarters," Mom says.

"So, wait," I say. "You actually think we're legitimate?"

"Absolutely," Dad says. "We couldn't have defeated Siphon or Tormentus without you. After the Berserker ambushed you in your treehouse, we knew it was time you had a safer, more state-of-the-art base to work from."

Well, he's right about that. After all, the Hangout is in Selfie's backyard. We were sitting ducks when the Berserker came back from the dead to attack us.

I'm in complete shock as I stare at our new headquarters. All I ever wanted is for my parents to think of us as a real superhero team. And now they do! This is the best day ever!

"There is one catch," Mom says. "Since you are all still minors, we've installed cameras throughout the facility so we can keep an eye on you from the Waystation. And no, Pinball, there aren't any cameras in the bathrooms."

"Oh, yeah," he says, turning beet red. "I forgot you can read minds."

Well, knowing my parents I'm not surprised our new headquarters comes with parental controls. But that's okay with me because we have our own freaking headquarters! How cool is that?

"This is amazing," I say. "Thank you so much!"

"Yeah, thanks," Selfie says, and everyone else gives their thanks as well.

"TechnocRat gets all the credit," Dad says. "He took down the old movie theater and built this just for you."

"Wow, thanks, TechnocRat," I say.

"It was my pleasure, kid," he says. "Besides, I figured I owed you one. So, are you ready for the grand tour?"

"I love grand tours!" Pinball exclaims.

"Why don't we turn the Distorter back on before we go inside?" Mom suggests. "Now that they know what the building really looks like, we don't need anyone else finding out about it too."

"Good point," TechnocRat says as he presses the button on the Distorter. The blue light comes back on and the Spotlight Theater reappears. "The Distorter will run 24-7 inside the building. There's no reason to ever turn it off."

"That's so cool," Night Owl says.

"Follow me," TechnocRat says.

As we walk to the entrance, I realize that everyone is here except for Grace. Why didn't she come? Maybe she's jealous. Well, she should be.

Suddenly, Selfie grabs my arm and whispers, "Epic, this is incredible. Now we have a big enough headquarters to grow our team."

"Yeah," I whisper back with a smile.

Selfie and I have been talking a lot about expanding Next Gen. The five of us—well, six including Dog-Gone—can only handle so many threats. It sure would be nice to add some new members to the team.

"The front door opens by facial recognition," TechnocRat says. "I've programmed it to read each of your faces and ours as well. Simply look into the ticket window like this, and—"

"Facial recognition confirmed," comes a mechanical, female voice. "Door opening."

"Oh, that's AVA," TechnocRat says. "AVA is short for Automated Virtual Assistant. AVA controls all of the systems inside the building. She can answer questions, make recommendations, and perform actions. She's programmed to respond to all of our voices. Isn't that right, AVA?"

"Yes, TechnocRat the Mighty," AVA responds.

"Heh, heh, oops," TechnocRat says, his white cheeks turning pink. "I guess I forgot to remove that from AVA's programming. Anyway, follow me."

We step inside and my jaw drops because the inside is just as impressive as the outside! First of all, the space is enormous. The walls are covered with TV monitors that are cycling through news channels from around the world. There's a huge recreation area to our right, with comfy sofas, a ping-pong table, a pool table, and an indoor basketball hoop. To our left is a modern kitchen with a fully stocked pantry, multiple dining tables, and a—

"Popcorn machine!" Pinball exclaims as he bounces into the kitchen. "Yes!"

"You like that?" TechnocRat asks. "I thought it would be nice to tie back to the history of the theater. Anyway, I call this floor the Rec Room. You can come down here to have fun and just be kids. If you need anything, just ask AVA and she'll have it delivered."

"Just keep in mind," Dad warns, "the bill comes to us, so please don't overdo it."

"Of course, you still have to load the dishwasher and take out the trash," TechnocRat says. "Now, who wants to see the second floor?"

"I do!" we all say at once.

We follow TechnocRat onto a large cargo elevator and he says, "AVA, second floor please."

"Yes, TechnocRat the Brilliant," AVA says.

"I'm sensing a theme here," Skunk Girl mutters.

The elevator stops on the second floor and we step into a long hallway that has a dozen doors on each side.

"This floor houses the dormitory," TechnocRat says. "Each room is identical and has everything you need if you have to stay overnight. There's a bed, a desk, and a private bathroom. Plus, you have plenty of extra rooms for guests. I figured you could each claim a room and decorate it however you wanted."

"Cool!" Pinball says.

Suddenly, the door on the far left opens, and, to my surprise, Grace steps out!

"Speaking of claiming rooms," Grace says. "This one is mine."

"Wait, what?" I blurt out. "What are you doing here? This is our headquarters."

"This facility is for all of our young heroes," Mom says. "Including Glory Girl."

"Whoa! Hang on," I say, turning to my parents. "I thought you said the cameras were the only catch?"

"Epic Zero," Dad says, "this headquarters is as much hers as it is yours."

"Are you kidding me?!" I exclaim. "Can't the 'Mighty and Brilliant' TechnocRat build her a separate headquarters somewhere else? Like, on Mars maybe?"

"Epic Zero…" Dad starts.

"It's okay, Epic," Selfie says, putting her hand firmly on my arm. "We're happy to share with her."

"You can say that again!" Pinball says, making googly eyes at Grace.

"Um, yuck," Grace says. "Well, thank you, Selfie. I'm glad one of you has manners. And for what it's worth, I'm happy to share my headquarters with you losers."

"*Your* headquarters?!" I exclaim.

"Glory Girl…" Mom warns.

"Just kidding," Grace says, patting me on the head. "Not all of you are losers."

"Okay, everyone," TechnocRat says, "why don't we see the third floor?"

I'm still stewing as we get back in the elevator and 'TechnocRat the Magnificent' shows us the third floor. There's a spacious Combat Room, just like the one on the Waystation, with white walls and a super high ceiling. And next to the Combat Room is another room filled with empty display cases.

"What's this room for?" Night Owl asks.

The others might be clueless, but I know exactly what this room is for.

"This is a Trophy Room, isn't it?" I ask.

"Correct," TechnocRat says. "Now you'll be able to display mementos from your own team missions."

Wow, that's awesome. I look inside one of the empty display cases. I've always dreamed of filling a room with our own trophies. I just never thought it would happen.

"Let's go to the fourth floor," TechnocRat says. "I think you'll be excited by what you find there."

We take the elevator again, and when we reach the fourth floor, 'TechnocRat the Incomparable' shows us something that blows my mind. To our left is a Mission Room with big, leather chairs and a circular conference table with the letters 'NG' engraved in the center.

"For 'Next Gen,'" TechnocRat says.

"Aw," Selfie says. "You're so thoughtful."

Then, I turn around and my eyes pop open wide. Across the hall is another room with a large, familiar-looking computer.

No. Freaking. Way.

"Is—Is that the Meta Monitor?" I ask.

"Yes!" TechnocRat says. "Well, actually it's a duplicate, but now you have your own Meta Monitor right here on Earth. I know. I rock."

I reach out and give TechnocRat a high paw. The whole headquarters is amazing but having our own Meta Monitor makes it even better!

"One more stop," TechnocRat says, beckoning us back to the elevator.

"Fifth floor, AVA," TechnocRat says.

"Oh, please, not again," Skunk Girl mutters, covering her ears.

"Yes, TechnocRat the Sensational," AVA responds.

"I think I'm gonna yack," Skunk Girl says.

We arrive on the top floor to find a fully functional Hangar! And that's not all, because parked inside is a very large jet that looks just like a Freedom Flyer, except, this one has the words "Gen-Jet" painted on its wings!

"You didn't?" I say to TechnocRat in disbelief.

"Oh, but I did," TechnocRat says. "That's your brand new Gen-Jet. I thought the name was kind of clever. It's got room for all of you."

"Even Pinball?" Skunk Girl asks.

"Hey!" Pinball exclaims.

"Even Pinball," TechnocRat answers.

"Thank you so much," I say, feeling overwhelmed. "This is way more than we ever could have imagined."

"You've earned it," Dad says. "This gives you all of the tools you need to be successful."

"And we're always here to help," Mom adds.

"Thanks," I say. "I—"

"Alert! Alert! Alert!" the Meta Monitor blares over the speakers. "Meta 3 disturbance. Repeat: Meta 3 disturbance. Power signature identified as Computron. Alert! Alert! Alert! Meta 3 disturbance. Power signature identified as Computron."

"Well, I guess everything works," Glory Girl says.

I look at my friends and we all nod.

"Do you mind if we take this one?" I ask.

"Not at all," Dad says. "Go get 'em, Next Gen."

We hop into the Gen-Jet, which has that unmistakable new-jet smell. I grip the steering wheel, hit the ignition button, and the Gen-Jet REVS with power.

"Now, how do we get out of here?" Pinball asks. "The Hangar doors are still closed."

"I think we ask AVA to open them," Selfie says.

"Right," I say. "Hey, AVA, can you open the Hangar doors?"

"Certainly, Epic Zero," AVA says, as the giant hangar doors slide open.

"Thank goodness," Skunk Girl says. "I was worried

TechnocRat programmed empty platitudes for you too."

"I guess I'll have to fix that," I say with a smile.

Then, I wave to the Freedom Force, power the jets, and we're off!

Meta Profile
The Freedom Force
Captain Justice
Class: Super-Strength
Meta :
Ms. Understood
Class: Psychic
Meta :
Glory Girl
Class: Flight
Meta :
Shadow Hawk
Class: None
Meta :
Epic Zero
Class: Meta Manipulator
Meta :
TechnocRat
Class: Super-Intellect
Meta :
Blue Bolt
Class: Super-Speed
Meta :
Master Mime
Class: Magic
Meta :
Makeshift
Class: Energy Manipulator
Meta :

TWO

I HAVE A SUPREME HEADACHE

Everything I've worked for is finally paying off.

The Freedom Force not only considers Next Gen to be legit, but they've also given us our very own headquarters! I can't believe it. All of my dreams are finally coming true! Well, almost all of my dreams. Having Grace hanging around our new headquarters is a bit of a nightmare, but I guess I can't win 'em all.

But I'm not going to complain, especially since we're flying to our next mission in our brand-new Gen-Jet! This is our time to shine. This is our opportunity to put Next Gen on the superhero map. This is our chance to show everyone what we can do.

"I've gotta pee," Pinball says.

Or maybe not.

"You're joking, right?" Skunk Girl asks.

"No," Pinball says. "I've had to go since we were blindfolded, but the new headquarters was so exciting I held it. But I don't think I can wait anymore."

"Well, you're gonna have to wait for at least another minute," I say, "because we're almost there."

"I'll… try my best," he says with a strained voice.

"Yo, boss-man," Skunk Girl says. "If he has an accident you're paying for my dry cleaning. I'm just sayin'…"

I roll my eyes when the Gen-Jet announces—

"Meta 3 signature at 0100."

I look down and see that we're flying over a large factory with giant smokestacks and a large sign on the roof that reads: CHEMICO. The parking lot is jammed with cars all heading for the exits. That's good news because the more people who leave, the fewer people we have to rescue.

"What is Chemico?" Night Owl asks.

"It's a chemicals company," I say. "I think they manufacture rare and dangerous chemicals."

"Of course, they do," Night Owl says sarcastically as she rolls her eyes.

"Hey, I don't think we ever got the full lowdown on this mission," Skunk Girl says. "Who's the bad guy and what are we doing here again?"

"Oh, sorry," I say, picturing Computron's Meta

Profile in my head. "He's called Computron, and he's an…"

Suddenly, I realize that in all of the excitement, I overlooked one important little detail. Computron is an android, which is basically a robot that looks human. And my powers don't work against robots!

"Epic, are you okay?" Selfie asks. "You just stopped talking."

"What? Oh, yeah, sorry," I say. "Computron is a Meta 3 android with Super Intelligence. He may look like a regular guy, but underneath his synthetic skin is a super-computer with an arsenal of deadly gadgets. He's a calculating killer, so we need to find him fast and stop him from doing whatever he's trying to do."

"Well, I don't know what he's trying to do," Night Owl says, pointing to our left, "but I know where he is."

I follow her outstretched arm and see plumes of black smoke pouring out of a shattered factory window.

Yep, that's him.

"I'm touching down," I say. "Get ready."

I land the Gen-Jet in front of the factory and pop open the hatch.

"I'll be back!" Pinball announces as he bounces out of the jet and around the side of the building.

"Can we change his name to 'Bladder Boy?'" Skunk Girl asks.

"So, what's the plan?" Selfie asks, looking at me.

Now there's a great question. I mean, I feel kind of

embarrassed. Despite our run-ins with robotic villains like Gigantox and the Meta-Busters, I realize I never told them about the limitations of my powers. I don't know why I didn't say anything. I guess I didn't want it to seem like I couldn't handle everything that came my way. But now I've learned that if we're going to be a great team then we need to share our strengths *and* weaknesses—including mine. So, it's time I came clean.

"Okay," I say, "first, there's something I have to tell you about my powers. You see—"

"I'm back!" Pinball shouts as he bounds around the corner. "What a relief."

"Yeah, comic relief," Skunk Girl quips.

"Okay, anyway," I say, "here's the deal. You see—"

BOOM!

We all duck as something huge explodes overhead, and when I look up I see giant chunks of rubble raining down on us!

"Got it!" Night Owl calls out.

Then, she forms a shadow shield over our heads. As debris POUNDS against Night Owl's shadow barrier, I open my mouth to issue orders, when—

THUD! The ground shakes, and when I look to our right, a tall, trim man with slicked-back hair and a blue jumpsuit is standing ten feet away! His cold, red eyes scan each of us in turn, like he's analyzing us. Then, I notice he's holding a canister of orange, swirling gas.

"Um, I'm thinking that's the guy," Skunk Girl says.

"Yep," I say, swallowing hard. "That's him alright."

"Miniature superheroes?" Computron says with an amused, mechanical-sounding voice. "How fascinating."

"Listen carefully, Computron," I say firmly, "because this is the only warning you're going to get. Hand over that canister and turn yourself in, or we'll drag you in piece by piece."

"How brave of you, Epic Zero," Computron says.

Huh? How does he know my name?

"Unfortunately," he continues, "your command does not synchronize with my objectives. This canister contains a unique chemical agent that will supercharge my motherboard and raise my capabilities to a new level. Besides, I have downloaded all available data on each of your abilities and calculated the probability of my victory in battle at 99.3%."

"That's a high number, right?" Pinball whispers.

"Yeah, dummy," Skunk Girl says. "But not for us."

"Prepare for elimination," Computron says. Then, he points his right arm at Night Owl, retracts his hand into his wrist, and replaces it with a long, metallic tube.

"Night Owl!" I yell. "Run!"

But before she can react, Computron shifts his aim to the ground beneath her feet.

FWOOM!

There's a huge explosion that blows me onto my tailbone, and when I look up, Night Owl is lying unconscious on her back! Then, Computron wheels on

Selfie and switches out his gun for a hook!

"No!" I call out.

FWOOP!

The hook shoots out of Computron's arm and wraps around Selfie's phone, yanking it out of her hand! Then, he whips her phone around and CLONKS her on the back of the head, knocking her to the ground.

"He's mine!" Pinball calls out as he bounces off the side of the building and ricochets toward Computron.

But the android holds his ground and—WHAM! Computron kicks Pinball so hard that he goes flying into the air and disappears over the horizon!

"Okay, boss-man," Skunk Girl says, "I'll distract him and you negate his powers. Hey, metal-head! Over here!"

"Skunk Girl, wait!" I call out, but she's already in motion, sending a powerful stink wave right at the android's face.

But Computron doesn't flinch. Instead, he calmly exchanges his hook for a hose and douses Skunk Girl in a thick, foamy substance.

"H-Help!" comes Skunk Girl's muffled cry as she slips to the ground. "I-I can't get this stuff off me!"

I step toward Skunk Girl when Computron suddenly wheels on me! I'm a sitting duck!

"Interesting," Computron says, his eyes spinning in his head like a slot machine. "My download shows no evidence of your powers working against an android enemy. You must be helpless against such adversaries."

O. M. G! He knows!

Suddenly, his eyes glow bright red.

He's gonna vaporize me!

"Don't worry, little fella," comes a voice from up high. "I'll save you."

Suddenly, an orange and black blur drops from the sky, and—KAPOW! Computron is pounded into the ground with incredible force! What was that? But before I can discover the answer, I see Computron's canister hurtling through the air!

My instincts kick in and I dive to catch it before it shatters on the ground and releases whatever dangerous chemical is trapped inside. But just as I'm about to grab it with my outstretched arms, a hand snatches it away.

"Oof!" I exclaim as I belly-flop hard onto the ground, knocking the wind out of me.

"You okay, little guy?" comes a kid's voice.

I roll over, and when I look up I see a masked kid smiling down at me with gleaming, white teeth. His jaw is perfectly square, his dimples are perfectly dimpled, and his black hair is perfectly curled in all the right places.

"Let me give you a hand," he offers.

As he pulls me up with a muscular arm, I take in his orange costume, black cape, and the letters 'KS' stretched across his broad chest. He's cradling the canister in his arm like a football, and as I get to my feet I realize I'm a full foot shorter than him.

"There you go," he says, his brown eyes sparkling

through his black mask. "I'm Kid Supreme." Then, he looks me up and down and says, "And you are?"

"Epic Zero," I say. When I look down I notice the front of my costume is covered with dirt. "Sorry, you probably didn't recognize me."

"Recognize you?" he says. "I've never heard of you. Well, it's a good thing I was flying by because you were in some major trouble."

Speaking of trouble, I look over and see Computron lying motionless in the middle of a five-foot-deep crater.

Wow, Kid Supreme absolutely clobbered him.

"Um, yeah," I say. "Thanks for your help."

"I'm sorry to be so blunt here, but you should really be more careful," Kid Supreme says. "Clearly, you were in way over your head. You could have been killed if I didn't come along when I did."

Um, excuse me?! I mean, the nerve of this guy! He has no clue who I am or what I've done for this planet!

"Do you even have powers?" he asks.

"Look, buddy," I say, "you wouldn't believe the powers I—"

"Epic?" comes Selfie's voice.

Holy cow! This guy was yapping so much that I forgot to check in on the team! Selfie is heading our way and Night Owl is cleaning the suds off of Skunk Girl. We just need to find Pinball.

"Oh, hi," Selfie says as she looks up at Kid Supreme. For a second, I think I see her cheeks turn pink.

"Hey there," Kid Supreme says, flashing a big, cheesy smile.

"What happened to him?" Selfie asks as she looks at Computron. "Epic, did you do that?"

"No, it was me," Kid Supreme says, flexing his giant bicep as he scratches the side of his head.

"Oh, wow," she says.

"Yeah," he says, puffing out his chest. "I know."

"Well, thanks for your help," I interject, "but we'll take it from here. Just hand over the canister and you can be on your way."

"Epic, hold on," Selfie says. She looks at Kid Supreme and says, "Excuse us for a second." Then, she pulls me to the side and whispers, "Listen, we want to expand our team and we don't have anyone with powers like his. He could really help us."

"Him?" I whisper. "No way."

"Why not?" she whispers.

"Because," I whisper. "That's why."

""That's not a reason," she whispers. "What's the problem?"

"Nothing," I whisper. "There's just something about him I don't like. I mean, who calls themselves 'Kid Supreme' anyway?"

"Fine," Selfie whispers, clearly annoyed. "For now."

I nod, and as we turn around, I say, "Sorry, we were just talking about—"

"That's okay," Kid Supreme says, interrupting me. "I

know what you were talking about and I'm not interested in joining your team."

"Wait," I say. "You heard us?"

"Of course, I did," Kid Supreme says. "Look, let's be honest here. Your team isn't at my level. I mean, the only way I'd even consider joining you is if I was the leader."

"What?!" I blurt out. "Are you kidding?"

"No," he says. "You need a real leader. Some of you, like her, have potential. But you need someone who knows what they're doing to bring it out."

"I know what I'm doing," I say, crossing my arms.

"Really?" Kid Supreme says. "Could have fooled me. Anyway, here's your canister." Kid Supreme hands it to Selfie. "Be careful with that. Well, it was nice saving you. See you around."

Then, he winks at Selfie and rockets into the air.

"Wow, who was that handsome guy?" Skunk Girl asks as she and Night Owl join us.

"No one we want to know," I answer.

Meta Profile
Next Gen
Epic Zero
Class: Meta Manipulator
Meta :
Dog-Gone
Class: Meta-Morph
Meta :
Night Owl
Class: Energy Manipulator
Meta :
Skunk Girl
Class: Energy Manipulator
Meta :
Selfie
Class: Magic
Meta :
Pinball
Class: Meta-Morph
Meta :

THREE

I CAN'T CATCH A BREAK

I'm so happy to be back in our new headquarters.

Before we left Chemico, we returned the canister of chemicals to the person in charge and then delivered Computron straight to Lockdown. Hopefully, we won't see his face again. And speaking of faces I never want to see again, you can add Kid Supreme to the list.

Sure, he saved my bacon. Even I can admit that. But to claim he's never heard of me? I mean, come on! I've saved the universe more times than he can count. Never heard of me, huh? Well, I'd never heard of him before today and now I'm sorry I have.

I didn't think anyone could have an ego bigger than Grace's, but he's proven me wrong! I mean, you have to have a pretty big head to call yourself 'Kid Supreme.' And what exactly is he 'Supreme' at anyway? If he called himself 'Kid Supremely Annoying' it would make a lot more sense.

Selfie seemed to take a shine to him though, and I could be wrong, but I think he liked her too. Sure, he's handsome, muscular, and dimpled, but he also has an obnoxious personality. I nearly exploded when he called me a lousy leader in front of Selfie. I know I wasn't at my best during the battle with Computron, but the nerve of that guy!

And to think, Kid Supreme said he'd only join our team if *he* was the leader. Well, that's great news because I'm not giving up the role any time soon. So, see ya around, sucker!

"Earth to Epic," comes Selfie's voice.

"Huh?" I say, turning to see her sitting beside me on the Rec Room couch.

"Finally," she says. "I've asked you five times if you wanted a drink but you're totally spaced out."

"Oh, sorry," I say, "I was just thinking about, um, things. Yeah, I'd love a drink. Thanks."

"Things, huh?" she says with a smirk as she heads into the kitchen. "You're not still thinking about Kid Supreme, are you?"

Drat. Busted.

"Um, maybe," I mutter.

"Well, don't worry about him," she says, grabbing

two water bottles from the fridge. "I think you're right."

"I am?" I say surprised. "Wait, about what?"

"That he's not a good fit for our team," she says. "Even if he does have amazing powers."

"And huge muscles," Skunk Girl adds from the ping pong table. "Don't forget about the muscles."

"Can you just serve the ball already?" Night Owl asks impatiently from the other side of the table.

"Hey, don't rush perfection," Skunk Girl says.

"So, wait a minute," I say to Selfie. "Are you saying you don't want him on our team?"

"No," she says, handing me a water bottle. "We can't have any lone wolves in this group. We're a team and teams work together. Besides, I didn't like the way he talked to you. He was way too arrogant."

"Really?" I say, my voice rising with excitement. "I mean," I say, lowering my voice, "yes, I agree."

COUGH! COUGH!

"Pinball, are you okay?" Selfie asks.

I turn to find him inhaling another tub of popcorn.

"Yep," he says with a thumbs up.

It took us a while to find Pinball after the Computron fight. That android kicked him so hard that he landed a few cities away. After surviving that, death by popcorn would be a ridiculous way to go.

"You should slow down, Pinball," Selfie says. "There's no need to eat it all now. The popcorn isn't going anywhere."

"Yeah, you're right," he says, pushing the tub away from him. "When I go to the movies, I always finish my popcorn before the previews end so I can get a refill. But I guess I don't have to do that here. It's so cool that our headquarters is inside an old movie theater. We should give it a nickname. How about… the Hideout?"

"We're not criminals, Pinball," Skunk Girl says.

"Okay," he says, "then how about the Fortress of Awesomeness? Or the Cool Cave? Or… the Yay Station? Get it? The Freedom Force has the Waystation, but we have the…" Suddenly, his enthusiasm fades as he looks at our faces. "No good, huh?"

"Horrible," Skunk Girl says. "Just horrible."

"How about 'The Beacon?'" Selfie suggests. "It kind of has a double meaning. A beacon is like a spotlight, so it pays homage to the Spotlight Theater's name, but a beacon is also a source of inspiration."

"Yeah, I kind of like that," Night Owl says.

"The Beacon," Skunk Girl says, trying it out. "It does have a nice ring to it."

"Yeah, it's okay," Pinball says with a shrug. "I mean, it kind of sounds like bacon but that's cool. I like bacon."

"Then that's it," I say. "The Beacon it is."

"Freedom Ferry arriving," AVA suddenly announces. "Would you like me to turn on visual monitoring?"

"What? Oh, yes, thanks," I say. Hmm, I wonder who it is? Maybe Mom and Dad are checking on us.

The monitors flicker on, showing an image of the fifth-floor Hangar as the Freedom Ferry parks inside. Then, the hatch opens and Grace and Dog-Gone hop out. Ugh, she's back. Well, at least she brought Dog-Gone. He's going to love it here.

I wait for them by the cargo elevator, and when it opens, Dog-Gone pounces, pinning me to the floor.

"Easy boy!" I say as he assaults me with licks.

"He's all yours now," Grace says as she saunters into the kitchen. "The rest of the Freedom Force are off-world on a mission. They left me behind in case they get into a jam and need help getting back. So, when I realized it was just me and your mutt up on the Waystation, I brought him down to you. I mean, I'm not cleaning up after him. And speaking of messes, you sure made a big one on that Computron mission. You looked like complete morons."

"Believe me," I say as I sit up, "we don't need any commentary from you. We know we screwed up."

"Yeah, well you know who didn't screw up?" she asks, grabbing a jelly donut from the pastry tray. "That kid who saved you, that's who. I don't know his name but you should get him on your team. Then you might actually look like you know what you're doing."

"We know what we're doing," I say firmly.

"Uh-huh," she says, stuffing her face.

Well, this co-living arrangement is going swimmingly. I wonder if I can trade her to the Rising Suns for some toilet paper?

"Anyway, did you see what's happening at the United Nations?" she asks.

"The United Nations?" I say.

"Yeah, the United Nations," she says. "You know, the UN, the international organization of countries who work together for world peace."

"I know what the UN is," I say. "What about it?"

"I was listening to the police scanner on the way down and there's big trouble brewing over there," she says. Then, she looks at the monitors and says, "Not that you'd know about it since all of your monitors are tuned into the Hangar."

She's right. Come to think of it, the monitors were off before AVA told us Grace was coming. It must be a technical glitch because they're supposed to be running all the time so we can stay on top of the news for any trouble. I'll have to let TechnocRat know.

"AVA," I command, "please turn on the news."

"Certainly, Epic Zero," AVA says.

Suddenly, all of the monitors switch on at once, showing news reports from around the world. And they're all featuring a familiar-looking glass skyscraper standing tall above a row of colorful, international flags.

It's the United Nations! I'd love to know what's going on but it's impossible to make out what's happening from all of the languages being spoken at the same time.

"AVA, just the American news, please," I say.

"Certainly, Epic Zero," AVA says.

"… the situation at the United Nations is growing more and more dire," a male reporter says. "One hundred and ninety three delegates, each representing their home country, had gathered here today for a meeting in the United Nations General Assembly Building. Now, all one hundred and ninety three are being held hostage by a group of teenaged Metas who are calling themselves the Game Changers."

"The Game Changers?" Skunk Girl says. "I've never heard of them."

Me neither. The camera zooms in and I see a bunch of costumed kids standing in front of the entrance. I don't recognize any of them, except for one red-headed boy who seems kind of familiar.

Where do I know him from?

"According to reports," the news anchor continues, "the leader of this band of teen Meta criminals will be addressing the United Nations momentarily. We hope to bring you this speech live if our crew can gain access to the building. Please stay tuned to our continuing coverage of this breaking story."

Stay tuned? Sorry, but we can't just sit here. Those delegates are in danger!

"Okay," I say, "I think it's time we put an end to this nonsense. Who's with me?"

"Count us all in," Selfie says. "If any of those

delegates get hurt it could lead to war."

"Before we go," Skunk Girl says, nodding over at Pinball, "maybe Bladder Boy here should go to the bathroom."

"Great idea!" Pinball says, bouncing off to the bathroom. "I'll meet you in the Hangar when I'm done."

The rest of us head for the elevator except for Grace.

"Aren't you coming?" I ask her.

"Me?" she says. "No, I need to stick around in case the Freedom Force needs me. Unless you don't think you can handle a bunch of teeny boppers?"

"We can handle them just fine," I say. "Keep an eye on Dog-Gone for me."

We hear CRUNCHING, and when we look over, Dog-Gone's snout is buried deep in Pinball's popcorn tub.

"I'm not watching that flea-bag," Grace says. "And just so you know, whatever messes he makes will be waiting for you when you get back."

Meta Profile

Computron

Name: INT-100X	Height: 6'4"
Race: Android	Weight: 190 lbs
Status: Villain/Active	Eyes/Hair: Red/Black

META 3: Super Intelligence
Extreme Analytical Skills
Extreme Data Processing
Body Contains Weapons

Observed Characteristics			
Combat 66			
Durability	54	Leadership	92
Strategy	100	Willpower	84

FOUR

I MEET THE COMPETITION

We reach New York City in no time.

I don't know what's happening inside United Nations Headquarters, but I do know this—whoever these Game Changers are, they're going to pay for taking the UN delegates hostage. I just hope we're not too late.

"UN Headquarters at eleven o'clock," Selfie says.

I nod and angle the Gen-Jet slightly left. I've been racking my brain about that red-headed kid since I saw him on the news, but it's just not clicking. I think I've flipped through the entire Meta Monitor in my brain but I still can't figure out who he is. Who knows, maybe he's buddies with Kid Supreme?

"Wow, look at all of those flags," Pinball says.

I look down at all of the international flags waving in unison in front of the UN. I have to admit, it is impressive. If the delegates were half as unified as their flags blowing together in the breeze, the world would be a better place.

I scan the area and realize that United Nations Headquarters isn't just that one skyscraper we saw on TV, but a vast compound with four different buildings. The delegates are being held in the General Assembly Building, which is actually the large, domed building next to the skyscraper.

"Where are we going to park this thing?" Skunk Girl asks. "Because it's awfully crowded down there."

She's right about that. Police cars are parked bumper to bumper in the driveway and news vans are lined up outside the gates. So, in other words, there's nowhere safe to land. Then, I spot a large fountain inside the compound and begin our descent.

"Um, Epic, what are you doing?" Selfie asks, gripping her armrests.

"Landing," I say.

"In the fountain?" she asks.

"Yep," I say.

Seconds later, we SPLASH down in the fountain. The landing is a little rougher than I'd like but at least we're on the ground. Now we need to get inside the General Assembly Building. I scan the perimeter and don't see any of the Game Changers around. However, we have attracted the attention of someone else—the cops!

"Night Owl," I call out as I pop the hatch, "can you get us over the police?"

"Roger that," Night Owl says as she grabs a shadow from the building and forms a ramp from the Gen-Jet to the front entrance of the General Assembly Building.

"Let's move!" I command as we hop onto the shadow slide and glide over the heads of the stunned police officers.

"Hey!" an officer shouts. "Freeze or we'll shoot!"

"Whoa! Hold your fire!" I call back without slowing down. At first, I'm disappointed they don't recognize us, but then I realize they probably think we're members of the Game Changers. "We're Next Gen! We're the good guys!"

"Next Gen? Who the heck is Next Gen?" I hear the police officer mutter.

"Where are the delegates?" Skunk Girl asks.

"Inside that domed building," Selfie says. "That's where they hold their meetings."

We jump off the shadow slide in front of the General Assembly Building and dash through the front doors. We stop in the empty lobby beneath a giant, spherical pendulum that's suspended from the cavernous ceiling. That's funny, there's no one h—

"Stop right there!" comes a girl's voice.

Suddenly, two costumed kids come racing through a

door! The girl is really tall and she's wearing a blue and red costume with the insignia of a white arrow pointing upward. The second kid is a wiry-looking boy in a black cat mask and matching black costume. I've never seen either of them before.

"I think you're the ones who need to stop," I say. "Let the delegates go or you'll be sorry."

"No dice, short stack," the girl says with a smirk. "I suggest you let yourselves out before we throw you out." Then, she extends her arms and grows in height until she's fifty feet tall!

"That's right," the boy says. "And if you need a hand, I've got plenty to spare." Suddenly, his entire body shimmers and he multiplies into two identical copies of himself! And then four, and then eight, and then sixteen!

"Next Gen, fan out!" I order.

"I've got the cat kid," Night Owls says. "Or kids."

"I'll take the giant," Skunk Girl says. "After all, the bigger the nostrils, the more stink they'll smell!"

"Hold it!" comes a voice from our right.

Great, reinforcements. But when I turn, I see that familiar red-headed kid running toward us. And behind him is a small, brown-haired kid who also looks vaguely familiar. I know them from somewhere.

But where?

"Thermo?" Selfie says. "Is that you?"

Thermo? Holy cow! That's Thermo! He tried out for our team back when Siphon made all of the grown-ups disappear from Earth. His powers were really limited then. But now he looks much more… confident.

"Yeah, it's me," Thermo says. "And I'm sure you remember Monsoon."

"Monsoon?" Pinball says. "You mean, the kid with the bucket?"

"Yeah," Monsoon says. "I don't need the bucket anymore. In fact, I think you'll be surprised by what I can do now."

"Same here," Thermo says. "I don't need to be near a thermostat to use my powers anymore."

"Um, that's great," I say. "But I'm confused. You both tried out for Next Gen because you wanted to be heroes. So, why are you hanging around with these criminals?"

"We're not criminals," the giant girl says. "We're heroes too. We're members of the Game Changers, the greatest Meta teens around."

"You'll have to prove that," I mutter.

"Anytime," she says with a wink. "Anyway, I'm Supersize and my friend here is—"

"—Copycat," all of the boy's identical bodies say at once.

"So, if you're heroes, then why are you holding the delegates hostage?" Night Owl asks.

"We're not holding them hostage," Copycat says.

"That's right," Supersize says. "We're just making sure that the entire world hears our message. And there's no better place to do that than right here at the United Nations."

"Well, that's some pretty weak justification," I say. "Holding people against their will is wrong, no matter the reason."

"Look, I understand where you're coming from but we're not here to hurt anyone," Thermo says. "We just need to deliver our message. In fact, why don't you come inside so you can hear from our leader yourself?"

"Your leader?" I say. "Who is your leader?"

"Her name is Harmony," Monsoon says, "and she's amazing. I think you'll really like her."

"Yeah," Thermo says. "Just come inside and listen. I know you'll like what she has to say."

"I don't know," I say. Then, I turn to my team. "What do you think?"

"Let's hear them out," Selfie says. "Then we'll see."

"Okay," I say. "We'll listen to your leader, but if you don't release everyone when she's finished then you'll have some real trouble on your hands. Got it?"

"Absolutely," Thermo says. "But I think you'll feel differently once you hear her message. Let's go inside. She's about to begin her speech."

Ugh, there's nothing I love more than a long-winded speech. Supersize shrinks back to normal size and Copycat collects himself as we head for the entrance to the General Assembly Hall. Thermo opens the double doors and my jaw drops because this is the most impressive conference room I've ever seen.

The space itself is ginormous. The room is circular, with a blue, domed ceiling dotted with lights, making it look like a starlit night sky. Hundreds of neatly organized tables line the floor as far as the eye can see, each designated for a specific country and occupied by its respective delegates. All of the chairs are facing a raised podium at the front of the chamber, and standing behind the microphone is a very pretty, blond-haired girl.

She looks serious as she gazes at her captive audience. She's wearing a white costume with the insignia of a dove on her top, and around her neck is a gold necklace holding a round, green pendant that looks like an eye.

"That's Harmony," Thermo says.

I gathered that. Unsurprisingly, we get lots of strange looks as we make our way into the hall.

"Why don't you sit back there?" Thermo suggests, pointing to some empty seats in the very back of the room. "We're going up on the podium."

Our seats are pretty far back, but thanks to the large monitors on either side of the podium, everyone has a close-up view of Harmony. We watch as Thermo and the others line up behind her. Then, she begins.

"Good afternoon," Harmony says, her confident voice echoing through the chamber. "We apologize for the delay, but we had to ensure that our message today is delivered not only to you, esteemed delegates of the

United Nations, but that it is also broadcast live to your home nations as well."

I didn't notice it before, but the podium is surrounded by dozens of cameras and news crews from all over the world.

"My name is Harmony," she continues, "and I am here today to introduce you to a new breed of hero. We are the Game Changers, a team of Meta-powered youths who have grown tired of watching the world being run by self-serving hypocrites, powermongers, and thieves."

Whoa! That's a pretty bold opening statement for a place like this. I look around, but to my surprise, not a single delegate is objecting or even batting an eye. They're all just sitting there, staring at Harmony.

"We believe there is no better place to share our message than here," she continues. "The United Nations is a global, multi-national initiative that was created to maintain international security, encourage international cooperation, and bring peace to the world. It is a noble ideal, but predictably, you have all failed miserably to deliver your stated objectives."

I look at Thermo and the others who are nodding in agreement.

"You have had more than enough time to get it right," Harmony continues. "You could have dismantled your weapons, decommissioned your armies, and put the welfare of your people first. But did you? We all know the answer. Which is why now is the time for change."

Change? What's that supposed to mean?

"From this day forward," Harmony continues, "the Game Changers will use our Meta powers not to fight crime, but to make the world a truly better place. To accomplish this Herculean task, we will assume control of all of the planet's resources. Under my guidance, we will disarm all weapons, disband all armies, and reallocate all resources to the people who need them most. Imagine, the hungry will be fed, the sick will receive care, and underdeveloped regions will finally obtain the financial resources they need. To accomplish this, we will ensure that we no longer operate as separate countries but as one world—a world operating in complete harmony."

Um, what? That sounds nice and all but how is she going to do that? I mean, she's never going to get everyone to agree to that.

But to my surprise, everyone in the room starts chanting, "HARMONY! HARMONY! HARMONY!"

"This is nuts," I whisper to Selfie.

"Yeah," she whispers, "but is it?"

"It is a beautiful vision, isn't it?" Harmony says, raising her hand to silence the audience. "I know we will get there, but I also know that change is not easy. After all, there will be those who wish to oppose us. There will be those who will want to cling to their power—to protect their turf. So, let me take this moment to provide a clear warning to anyone who attempts to stand in our way. There will be zero tolerance for criminals, oppositionists, or terrorists—and that includes Metas. Join us if you wish, but if you stand in our way you will be dealt with, and your punishment will be severe."

I swallow hard. Did she just say 'zero' tolerance?

For some reason, I feel like she's talking to me.

"Now is the time for action," she says. "For those of you in this room, take this message back to your leaders and convince them to lay down their arms. For those watching from home, take comfort in knowing the Game Changers are here—and the world is about to change for the better."

Then, Harmony raises her arms and there's a bright, white FLASH! And when my eyes finally blink clear, Harmony and the Game Changers are gone!

Meta Profile
The Game Changers
Harmony
Class: Unknown
Meta :
Supersize
Class: Meta-Morph
Meta :
Copycat
Class: Meta-Morph
Meta :
Thermo
Class: Energy Manipulator
Meta :
Monsoon
Class: Meta-Morph
Meta :

FIVE

I GET INTO A HEATED ARGUMENT

Harmony is everywhere.

After her stint at the United Nations, it seems like I can't turn around without seeing her face on TV, hearing her voice on the radio, or scrolling through replays of her speech on social media. But strangely, instead of the usual negative coverage you'd see after a controversial speech like that, everyone seems to be on Harmony's side!

Am I missing something here?

Sure, she had some great things to say about helping people, but did everyone just miss the part where she said she's taking over the world? So, while everyone else is bowing down to her, I'm poking through our new Meta Monitor at the Beacon.

I've probably tried over a hundred search queries but I still can't find out anything about Harmony. I've looked her up by name, variations of her name, synonyms of her name, hair color, eye color, height, voice records, and possible associations with other Metas. The result—nada.

No identity, no Meta Profile.

The Meta Monitor has struck out, which makes me think there's even more going on here. Unfortunately, I have no leads so I'm fresh out of ideas. And I've been at this for hours.

I try getting up but I'm trapped by a snoozing, eighty-five-pound German Shepherd who is lying across my lap. I keep telling him that he's not a lap dog but he doesn't listen. Of course, if there was food then—

"What's up?" comes a familiar voice, startling me.

"Grace, please," I say, my heart pounding. "Can you stop sneaking up on me like that?"

"I wasn't sneaking," Grace says, "I just woke up from a nap to see if there were any messages from Mom and Dad and saw you sitting here. So, did you handle that UN thing?"

I look at her innocently smiling face.

"So, are you saying you haven't seen anything that's been happening?" I ask.

"Um, no," she says. "I just told you I was sleeping."

"Right," I say. Well, now I know why Dog-Gone was whining to go out when we got back. "There's something you need to see. Dog-Gone, get up."

It takes all of my strength to nudge him off my lap. Then, I lead Grace into the Mission Room, sit down at the terminal, and pull up Harmony's speech. I watch Grace's mouth open wider and wider as she watches the replay.

"Who is this girl?" she asks when it ends.

"That's what I'm trying to find out," I say. "But she's not in the Meta Monitor. It's like she came out of nowhere."

"Well, with Metas that's not unusual," Grace says. "Do you remember the Electric Heel? He was just a shoe salesman until he got hit by lightning and went bonkers."

"Yeah, but this feels different," I say. "I get the sense that whoever Harmony is, she's been planning this for a long, long time."

<SQUAWK> "Epic?" comes Selfie's voice over the intercom. "Epic, are you there?"

"What's up?" I ask, pushing the intercom button.

"We were heading to the Combat Room when the elevator doors closed on Pinball," she says. "We've been trying to get AVA to release him but she's not responding."

AVA again? What's up with this virtual assistant? Don't get me wrong, I appreciate everything that TechnocRat did, but I think he forgot to finish the wiring or something.

"Okay, what floor is he stuck on?" I ask.

"Third floor," she says. "Can you meet us here?"

"Yep, on my way," I say. Then, I turn to Grace and say, "I've gotta go."

"Sounds like it," she says. "I'm going to do some digging to see what I can find out about Harmony."

"Good luck," I say, heading for the stairs, "because I couldn't find anything."

Dog-Gone follows me downstairs to the next level. I guess he's had enough of hanging out with Grace—not that I blame him. When we exit the stairwell, I see Selfie, Night Owl, and a smirking Skunk Girl. And when I look at the elevator, I see the top half of Pinball sticking out of the doors.

"Well, you don't see that every day," I remark.

"Just be thankful you're standing on this side of the elevator," Skunk Girl says.

"Very funny," Pinball says. "Now can someone please get me out of here?"

"I tried opening the doors with my powers but they're stuck," Night Owl says. "I didn't want to break anything."

"Do you see the respect I get?" Pinball asks. "She'd rather save the doors than me."

"Hey, it's a new place," Night Owl says with a shrug.

"AVA?" I call out. "Can you please open the elevator doors?" There's silence. "AVA?"

"Yes, Epic Zero," AVA finally responds.

"Well, at least she talks to you," Selfie says.

"Pinball is stuck in the elevator," I say. "Can you

open the doors?"

"Certainly, Epic Zero," AVA says.

There's a DING and the doors spring open.

"Whoa!" Pinball says, as his weight rolls him forward and he smushes Skunk Girl.

"Get off, you moron!" Skunk Girl yells.

"Sorry," Pinball says, getting to his feet. "Kind of."

"Well, now that that's over," Selfie says, "we were heading to the Combat Room to get in some practice. Do you want to join us?"

"Sure," I say. "That sounds like a great idea. I'd love to blow off some steam right now. What training module do you want to use?"

"Something basic," Selfie says as we enter the stark, white Combat Room. "After our last outing, I think we need to practice getting in sync with each other."

"Great idea," I say. "AVA, please load training module SS34."

"Certainly, Epic Zero," AVA replies. "Module loading."

Well, this should be interesting. On the Waystation, GISMO runs the Combat Room. But here, AVA controls everything. Hopefully, what happened to Pinball was just a one-time glitch or we could have some serious problems.

Just then, the room transforms into a lush forest, and we're surrounded by four gigantic rock creatures!

"Okay, here we go," I say. "Everyone stand back-to-back in a tight circle."

"These guys are huge!" Pinball exclaims. "Look at the size of their fists! Only Skunk Girl's head is bigger!"

"Ha, ha," Skunk Girl says sarcastically. "Well, they're not bigger than your—"

"Enough!" Selfie yells. "We're trying to work as a team here. What's the call, Epic?"

"Let's split up and practice combination tactics," I say. "Night Owl, you work with Pinball and Skunk Girl to take out the ones on the left. Selfie and I will take the ones on the right."

"You got it," Night Owl says. "Let's go you two."

"Fine," Pinball and Skunk Girl say reluctantly.

"Ladies first," I say to Selfie with a gracious sweep of my arm. "You suggest the combos."

"Why, thank you, sir," she says with a curtsey. "Should we try the good ol' freeze and squeeze tactic?"

"Sounds perfect," I say.

"Great," she says. Then, she pulls out her phone and holds it up to the first rock creature. "Hey, say cheese!"

I turn my head as her magic phone FLASHES, and when I look back the rock creature is standing stock still with its eyes glazed over. Okay, Selfie delivered the 'freeze,' now it's my turn to deliver the 'squeeze.'

I reach out and duplicate Night Owl's power. Then, I grab a shadow from beneath a tree, wrap it around the creature's waist, and cinch it tight. THOOM! I protect us with a shadow shield as rocks explode everywhere.

"Nice," Selfie says. "Now for tactic number two. How about decoy and destroy?"

"Okay," I say. "But be careful."

"I'm always careful," she says with a smile. Then, she runs in front of the second rock giant and waves her arms, attracting its attention. "Yo, rocky, over here!"

She's done her job, now it's time to do mine. This time, I grab Pinball's Meta energy and pull it in. Suddenly, my entire body swells up like a balloon!

"Um, Epic?" Selfie calls out as the rock giant raises its massive fist. "You are gonna destroy, right?"

"Coming!" I shout. Great, now how does Pinball do this again? I take a little hop and bounce off the ground like I was shot out of a rocket! Whoa! I SLAM into one tree, RICOCHET off another, and head straight for the rock monster! I close my eyes and—

SLAM!

The collision is massive and rocks fly everywhere as my body ping-pongs from tree to tree! I finally remember to drop Pinball's power and land in a heap on the forest floor. Wow, I'm super dizzy. I don't know how Pinball can even focus when he's using his power, but then again, it probably explains a lot.

"Epic, are you okay?" Selfie asks as she runs over.

"If there are three of you then I'm fine," I say, getting to my feet. "How are the others doing?"

"They're just finishing up," Selfie says. "It was a great idea to have Pinball and Skunk Girl work together.

Hopefully, they'll start getting along better. And speaking of getting along, what did you think of Harmony's message? I wanted to talk to you about it but you kind of disappeared when we got back to the Beacon."

She's right about that. We were all kind of speechless on the ride home and I went right to the Meta Monitor when we got back.

"Well, maybe it's just me, but I'm always a little concerned when someone says they want to take over the planet," I say. "She kind of reminds me of the Skelton Emperor."

"Oh, I don't think Harmony is anything like him," Selfie says, waving her hand dismissively. "She doesn't want power for power's sake. She just wants to change the world for the better. I actually liked what she had to say."

"You did?" I ask, surprised.

"Yes, I did," she says firmly, crossing her arms. "I mean, I've been thinking about it a lot. Sure, we use our powers to put bad guys in jail, but are we really doing anything to change the world? I mean, after hearing what she had to say, I feel like we're just maintaining the status quo. A villain shows up here and we deal with it. Another villain shows up there and we deal with that too. But are we really doing anything to help people live better lives? To help them get what they need? We have all of these amazing gifts, but do we really use them in the best way possible?"

"Are you serious?" I ask, my voice rising. "That's not our job. We're superheroes, not the Peace Corps. We protect people from evil. We help maintain law and order. That's what this job is all about."

"Don't be so narrow-minded," Selfie says sharply. "There's no rule book. No one said it has to be that way. We can do whatever we want with our powers. Especially if it creates more good in the world."

We stare at each other in silence. Selfie and I have never argued before and it doesn't feel good. I mean, there's nothing wrong with what she's saying, I just don't agree with the way Harmony is going about it. But it seems like we're on opposite sides of this one.

"Okay, Boss-man," Skunk Girl says, breaking the tension. "We're all done. Two more rock piles are ready for delivery. Um, what's going on over here?"

"Nothing," Selfie and I say at the same time.

"Well, okay then," Skunk Girl says awkwardly.

"I'll stop the simulation," I say. "AVA, end program."

"Training module ended, Epic Zero," AVA says.

But as the forest scene fades, we suddenly hear—

"Alert! Alert! Alert!" the Meta Monitor blares. "Meta 3 disturbance. Repeat: Meta 3 disturbance. Power signature identified as Alligazer."

I freeze.

"Alert! Alert! Alert!" the Meta Monitor repeats. "Meta 3 disturbance. Repeat—"

But as it keeps going, I don't even hear the words because I'm in a complete state of shock. I mean, did it really just say, 'Alligazer?' As in, *the* Alligazer? You know, the Meta creep who nearly killed Makeshift—all because of me.

"Let's go!" Pinball says as the team races for the exit.

"Epic?" Selfie says as they reach the door. "Aren't you coming?"

"Uh, yeah," I hear myself say. "I'm right behind you."

But as they disappear through the doorway, I realize I'm still standing in the same place.

Meta Profile

Alligazer

▯ Name: Anton Bing	▯ Height: 6'3"
▯ Race: Human	▯ Weight: 225 lbs
▯ Status: Villain/Active	▯ Eyes/Hair: Yellow/Bald

META 3: Energy Manipulator
▯ Extreme Petrification
▯ Extreme Agility
▯ Can Cling to Surfaces

Observed Characteristics			
Combat 85			
Durability	90	Leadership	55
Strategy	69	Willpower	87

SIX

I SENSE TROUBLE BREWING

I haven't been this freaked out in a long time.

And can you blame me? I can't believe we're speeding in the Gen-Jet to face Alligazer, one of the most dangerous, cold-blooded killers around! The thought of staring into his beady, yellow eyes and ending up as a statue has me petrified—literally!

The last time I saw Alligazer was a disaster. I chased him all by myself into the Keystone City sewer system which was a huge mistake. He toyed with me for a while before he escaped, but on his way to freedom he turned Makeshift into a statue—and it was all my fault! The only reason Makeshift is alive today is because Order and Chaos did me a favor after I unwittingly restored their existence by destroying Ravager.

I was lucky I survived my first encounter with Alligazer. But now I'm about to face him again and this time I'm bringing my whole inexperienced team! I wish we could sit this one out, but the Freedom Force is still off-world and Alligazer is too dangerous for the police to handle alone.

"Who is this villain again?" Night Owl asks.

"His name is Alligazer," I say, trying to sound calm. "He's a Meta 3 Energy Manipulator who can turn people to stone with a glance. So, whatever you do, don't look into his eyes or he'll petrify you, and then, well, that's it."

"You mean, 'that's it' as in, 'that's it' you're… dead?" Pinball asks, swallowing hard.

"As a doornail," I say.

"Great," Skunk Girl says. "Is there anything else we need to know?"

"Yeah," I say. "He's incredibly agile and can climb up walls and see in the dark."

"Well, he sounds lovely," Skunk Girl mutters.

"So, what's the plan?" Selfie asks.

"According to what I heard on the police scanner," I say, "they've cornered him in an abandoned warehouse but they can't get close enough to take him down. I think our best bet is to take him by surprise."

"I love surprises," Pinball says. "Once, for my birthday, my parents got me a seven-layer cake with a chocolate pudding filling and rainbow sprinkles that—"

"Right," I say, ignoring him as he chatters on in the

background. "Anyway, here's what I'm thinking. Night Owl, you provide shadow cover while I negate his powers. Then, the rest of you can move in to knock him out."

"Oh, I love knocking people out," Skunk Girl says, cracking her knuckles.

"—and then I ate the whole thing," Pinball finishes.

I take a deep breath. Boy, I hope this works.

"Look, there's the warehouse," Night Owl says, pointing at a large building with busted windows and a crumbling, brick exterior. "Hey, what's up with those police officers? They're not moving!"

As we fly over the warehouse, I see my worst fears have been realized. Dozens of police officers are frozen in place! Some are pointing their guns while others are reaching for their weapons, but they've all been turned to stone! Suddenly, I'm brought right back to my first meeting with Alligazer at the bank. I vividly remember all of those innocent people he turned to stone—the woman talking on her cell phone, the man looking up from his paper. I can't let that happen to my friends.

"Hang on," Selfie says, pointing down. "Whose jet is that?"

Jet? What jet? But as we glide over the building, I see a sleek, silver jet parked in the back. On its hood are the bold, red letters 'GC.'

"GC?" Pinball says. "What does that stand for?"

"Good Christmas?" Skunk Girl offers.

"No," Selfie says, "that stands for—"

BOOM!

The warehouse roof explodes and I pull up hard on the yoke to avoid the flying debris. What caused that? But when I look down I see the top half of Supersize emerging from the building—and she's growing bigger and bigger!

"The Game Changers!" Selfie calls out. "What are they doing here?"

My first thought is that they must be working with Alligazer! But when I circle, I notice that Supersize is wearing a pair of mirrored glasses! Why didn't I think of that? When Alligazer looks into those lenses, he'll be staring back at himself!

So, if Supersize is protecting herself from Alligazer, then she must be trying to catch him too! Suddenly, I spot a green figure with a long tail scampering out of the building. That's him!

"I'm landing so hold on tight," I say, touching down right in front of the fleeing criminal. "Okay, let's get him! And remember, don't look at his eyes!"

I pop the hatch, but before we can get out, an army of Copycats rushes past our Gen-Jet and surrounds Alligazer, blocking his escape.

"Monsoon, now!" Supersize calls out.

Just then, a powerful wave of water appears out of nowhere and CRASHES down on Alligazer, knocking him off his feet.

"Thermo, go!" Supersize orders.

Suddenly, it gets so cold my teeth start chattering. Then, solid ice starts forming all over Alligazer's soaking-wet body, literally stopping him cold!

Wow. I have to admit, I'm impressed by how easily the Game Changers captured Alligazer. I mean, he even got away from the Freedom Force.

"Oh, hi, Next Gen," Thermo says nonchalantly as he steps out from behind what's left of the warehouse. "See, I told you we got better."

"You sure did," Pinball says.

"It's great you caught him," I say, "but why are you even here?"

"We're implementing our zero-tolerance policy," Thermo says. "Unlike other Metas, we're not letting notorious villains roam free until they inevitably cause problems. Instead, we're proactively hunting down anyone who poses a threat to our objectives—just like our buddy Alligazer here."

"So, now that you have him, I guess you'll be taking him to Lockdown, right?" Selfie asks.

"Nope," Supersize says as she shrinks down to normal height. "That's the old way of thinking. Lockdown isn't necessary anymore."

"What?" I say. "Of course, Lockdown is necessary. It's the only place that can safely hold these deranged Meta villains. Without Lockdown, they'll just break out of a regular prison."

"We don't believe in prisons," Copycat says as he merges back into one body. "We have a different way of dealing with bad guys. And our solution is final."

"Final?" Skunk Girl says. "What does that mean?"

"I'd be happy to show you," comes a girl's voice.

I spin around to find Harmony standing behind me with her hands on her hips. As she stares at me with her bright, blue eyes, I feel myself smiling for some reason, but then I quickly regain my senses. She may look like a hero, but there's something about her I don't trust.

"I think I'm in love," Pinball sighs.

I ignore Pinball and ask Harmony, "So, what exactly does 'final' mean?"

"Watch and learn," Harmony says, striding past me. "Thermo, please thaw the villain."

"Whoa, hold on there," I say. "You can't just thaw out Alligazer. He'll slither out of here before you blink. You're lucky you captured him in the first place."

"It wasn't luck, kid," Supersize says, pounding her fist into her other hand. "I can prove it to you firsthand if you'd like?"

"No, Supersize," Harmony says. Then, she stares into my eyes and says, "You call yourself a hero. Do you want peace in this world? True peace? Everlasting peace?"

"Of course, I do," I say, swallowing hard. Suddenly, I feel uncomfortable. It's like she's studying me—evaluating me—determining if I'm on her side or not. "But not at any cost," I add.

"I see," she says, her lips pursing.

That's when I notice the eye amulet around her neck. The amulet itself is circular in shape, rimmed with gold, and hanging by a gold chain. The human-sized eye in the center looks like it's made of green marble.

"Let me show you how *we* deal with criminals," she continues, putting on a pair of mirrored glasses. "Then, you can decide if our methods are more effective than those you have used in the past. Thermo?"

"My pleasure," Thermo says, raising his hands.

Suddenly, the air goes from chilly to sauna hot, and the ice encasing Alligazer begins to melt.

"Get ready, team," I whisper. "As soon as he thaws out he's gonna make a break for it."

I'm on high alert as the ice begins to melt. First, Alligazer bends a finger. Then, he flexes his tail. Seconds later, all of the ice has melted into a pool of water beneath his feet! It takes a moment for Alligazer to get his bearings, but before he can take off—

"Relax, friend," Harmony says calmly.

"Friend?" Alligazer says, looking at her confused. "I don't even know you."

"Oh, but you do know me," Harmony says. "I'm the voice inside your head—the one who helps you, the one who makes you feel safe. The one you trust."

Alligazer's face softens and his stance relaxes. I don't know what's going on here but Alligazer isn't turning her to stone. Instead, it seems like he's captivated by her!

"You have committed serious crimes against humanity," Harmony continues. "You have murdered hundreds for your own personal gain. Isn't that so?"

"Yes," Alligazer says.

Whoa! She just made him admit to his crimes!

"You are a danger to society," Harmony says, "and you are past the point of rehabilitation. Is that correct?"

"Yes," he says again.

"It is time for you to pay for your crimes," she says. "Look into my glasses and activate your powers. Do what you know must be done."

"Hey, wait a second," I say, stepping forward, but Thermo and Supersize hold me back.

As Alligazer stares at his reflection in Harmony's mirrored glasses, his eyes begin to glow. And then—CRRRAAACCCKKKLLLEEE!

I can't believe it! He's turned himself to stone!

"Y-You killed him!" I shout.

"No," Harmony says, removing her glasses. "He did that to himself, didn't he? And that is the final solution."

"That's murder!" I yell.

"That's justice," Harmony responds. "Did you forget about his victims? Shouldn't he be held accountable for their murders? Would putting Alligazer in Lockdown provide the justice his victims truly deserve?"

"I have to admit, she kind of has a point there," Skunk Girl says.

"We are operating in a new world," Harmony says,

"and we will not allow the innocent to suffer at the hands of those who would willingly do them harm."

"It's okay, Epic Zero," Thermo says, putting his hand on my shoulder. "The world will be better for it. You'll see."

"Yeah, until she does that to someone who's a good person but doesn't agree with her," I quip.

"An interesting suggestion," Harmony says as she looks into my eyes. "Are you volunteering?"

"Um, no," I say.

"I didn't think so," she says. Then, she looks at my team and says, "There are hundreds of Meta criminals like Alligazer who are still on the loose. We could use your help to bring them to justice. Will you join us? Will you be part of the Game Changers?"

"No way!" I scoff. "We're not interested in joining your team. We're with Next Gen. Right team?" But when I glance at my friends, they look unsure. "Um, team?"

"That's right," Selfie finally says to Harmony. "We're with Next Gen."

"Very well," Harmony says with a smile. "Perhaps another time. Game Changers, we must go. There is much left to do."

Then, she turns and walks toward their jet. As we watch the Game Changers board and take off, I know we'll be running into them again soon.

And when we do, I suspect it won't be good.

Meta Profile

Harmony

Name: Unknown	Height: 5'1"
Race: Human	Weight: 112 lbs
Status: Hero/Active	Eyes/Hair: Blue/Blonde

META ?
Unknown
Unknown

Observed Characteristics			
Combat ?			
Durability	?	Leadership	?
Strategy	?	Willpower	?

SEVEN

I SHOULD NOT ANSWER THE DOOR

Everything is off.

We're back at the Beacon, and no one has said a word since our encounter with the Game Changers. We're all spread out in different parts of the Rec Room, lost in our thoughts. In fact, it's so quiet I actually miss Pinball and Skunk Girl sniping at each other.

Everyone is still processing what just happened. Harmony showed us what her 'zero tolerance policy' was all about, which is basically her playing the role of judge, jury, and executioner. In the case of Alligazer, she convinced him to turn himself into a statue, ending any threat he posed.

I don't know what Harmony's powers are, but based on what I just witnessed, I'd guess she's a Psychic—and a powerful one at that. What she made Alligazer do to himself was disturbing, but that's not the only thing that's bothering me.

When Harmony invited our team to join the Game Changers, it seemed like I was the only one against the idea. For a second there, it looked like Selfie and the others were seriously considering it. But I don't know if that's how they really felt, or if Harmony was influencing them with her powers.

I don't know what to think.

Meanwhile, every news station around the world is airing continuous Harmony coverage. It seems like everything she promised is actually coming true. Countries are dismantling their nuclear weapons, warring nations are sitting down to negotiate peace, and tons of food has been redistributed to impoverished regions. It's like the entire world is working together for once.

It's amazing. Yet, two conflicting thoughts keep colliding in my brain. One, Harmony is doing remarkable things. And two, Harmony is incredibly dangerous.

The thing is, I seem to be the only one thinking this way. Just then, I see something on one of the monitors that piques my interest. Thousands of people have gathered in New York City, and they're carrying banners with Harmony's name and image on them.

What's going on?

"AVA, please only play monitor seven," I say. "And turn up the volume."

"Certainly, Epic Zero," AVA says, as the other TV monitors switch off and the volume on monitor seven increases.

"… people are calling themselves Harmonites," the male news reporter says. "They are part of a new movement called Harmonyism, named, of course, for Harmony, the leader of the Game Changers. Many of these people have traveled hundreds of miles to show their support for Harmony and her noble mission for true world peace. This demonstration in New York City is the first of many that will be happening across the globe. Let's try to speak to one of the participants to gain more insight into this spectacular show of support. Sir? Excuse me, sir? May I ask you a few questions?"

"Yeah, yeah, of course," a mustached man says, lifting his sign and smiling for the camera. His sign reads: Harmony for President!

"Sir, why have you come out here today?" the reporter asks.

"That's simple," the man answers. "I want real peace, just like everyone else here."

"Yes, of course," the reporter says. "Can you share your thoughts about our new hero, Harmony?"

"Oh, wow," the man says. "She's, well, different in all of the best ways. She's the first Meta I've ever really believed in. I mean, she's not like all of those other heroes who pay lip service to making the world a better place. She's actually doing it. Harmony for President!"

Lip service?

"Well, there you have it," the reporter says as the man rejoins the crowd. "Harmony is the first hero who is truly making the world a better place."

O. M. G! What's he talking about? What about all of those times the Freedom Force saved the world? Or even Next Gen?

Just then, something wet licks my cheek.

"Yuck," I say. I wipe my face as Dog-Gone puts his big paws on my lap. "Don't tell me you're a Harmonite too?"

Suddenly, Dog-Gone's ears perk up and he BARKS so loudly my ear drums ring.

"What's wrong with you?" I ask, rubbing my ears.

KNOCK! KNOCK! KNOCK!

The noise startles me. I look around for its source and realize that someone is knocking on our front door!

"Who could that be?" Skunk Girl asks.

"A door-to-door salesman?" Night Owl says.

"Or maybe someone is here to catch a movie," Pinball says.

"Maybe," I say, "but why here? This theater has been closed for decades. AVA, give us a visual feed of the front door."

"Certainly, Epic Zero," AVA says.

All of the monitors flicker back on and show an image of a familiar-looking, muscle-bound kid standing outside our front door. Oh, no.

"That's Kid Supreme," Night Owl says. "What's he doing here?"

"Who cares?" Skunk Girl says. "Let him in. It's about time we had someone dreamy around here."

"Hey, what's that supposed to mean?" Pinball asks, looking a little dejected. "He might be tall, dark, and handsome, but you don't need all of that to be dreamy. Um, is anyone gonna back me up on that? Anyone?"

"AVA, is the Distorter still working?" I ask.

"Yes, Epic Zero," AVA says. "It is still functioning."

"Then how did he know we're here?" I ask rhetorically. With the Distorter running, the Beacon should look like a rundown movie theater.

KNOCK! KNOCK!

"Come on, open the door!" Kid Supreme shouts. "I know you're in there!"

I look at the monitor and see Kid Supreme leaning against the door and waving at the camera.

"I think we should let him in," Night Owl says. "Clearly, he knows we're here."

"No way," I say. "If we ignore him then maybe he'll go away."

"Look, Epic," Selfie says, "I know you don't like him but I don't think he's going away. And we're certainly not going to keep our secret headquarters a secret for long if he decides to bust through our front door."

Ugh, she's right. I don't know how Kid Supreme found our headquarters, but he doesn't seem like the type who gives up easily. So now, on top of everything else, I have to deal with this too.

"Fine, I'll get the door," I say, standing up. "Dog-Gone, get behind me and look menacing."

Dog-Gone nods and follows me to the front door.

Then, I take a deep breath and open it.

Kid Supreme smirks when he sees me, and before he can open his big mouth, I say, "No thank you, we don't need any vacuum cleaners." But before I can shut the door, he blocks it with his hand and says—

"Hey, sorry about the last time we met."

Wait, what?

"Epic, why don't you invite him in?" Selfie suggests with an encouraging nod.

"Great idea," Skunk Girl adds as she fixes up her black-and-white hair. "Let's do that."

Kid Supreme's eyebrows arch as I stare into his eyes.

"Please, come in, if you must," I say coldly as I open the door.

As he steps inside I hear panting, and when I turn around Dog-Gone is wagging his tail excitedly as Kid Supreme scratches him behind the ears.

"Some guard dog you are," I mutter.

"Nice crib," Kid Supreme says, looking around.

"Yeah, about that," I say. "Perhaps you can enlighten us as to how you knew we were here?"

"Oh, let's just say that I have my ways," he says suspiciously. "However, I'm impressed. For a bunch of rookies, this headquarters is way cooler than I thought."

"Rookies?" Pinball says. "We're not rookies."

"Sorry, I wasn't trying to offend you," Kid Supreme says. "But let's be honest, you guys didn't exactly knock it out of the park against Computron."

"Just to be clear," I say, "we would have taken him down without your help."

"Uh-huh," he says. Then, he looks at Selfie, flashes his pearly whites, and says, "Hey there."

"Hi," Selfie says, rolling her eyes.

"Well, a big 'hey there' from me too," Skunk Girl says, waving awkwardly. "Yoo-hoo, hi. Um, over here."

"So, now that you've found us, what can we help you with?" I ask. "Are you here to borrow some sugar or something? I can get it and then I'll show you the way out."

"No," he says with a laugh. "And I'm not here for you to help me. I'm here to help you."

"Really?" I say. "And how's that?"

"By joining your team," Kid Supreme says casually while smoothing out his black cape.

What? No. Freaking. Way.

"Sorry, but we don't have any openings at the moment," I blurt out. "Why don't you join Harmony and the Game Changers? I hear they're looking for new members."

"Yeah, she tried to recruit me," he says, "but I turned her down. She's a little too starry-eyed for me."

Well, hang on now. I'm shocked. That's the first sensible thing he's said.

"After she left, it got me thinking," he continues. "I realized it might be nice to work with some other kids. You know, to have some, well, friends. After all, it's lonely at the top. So, I'm here to join the team."

"As the leader?" Selfie asks.

"Nah," he says. "I don't need to be the leader. At least, not yet."

"Yeah? Well, you also don't need to be on our—"

"Epic," Selfie interjects. "Let's huddle up for a minute. Excuse us, Kid Supreme."

Kid Supreme smiles as I join the others.

"No," I whisper. "And besides, didn't you say you didn't want any 'lone wolves' on the team?"

"Yes," Selfie whispers, "but he seems sincere. I think he really wants to be part of our team. Look, I admit he's arrogant, but he could be a big help."

"He could be annoying," I whisper back.

"Yeah, that's my job," Pinball whispers.

"And you do it so well," Skunk Girl whispers.

"I think we should let him join," Night Owl whispers. "He has powers none of us have."

"Right," I whisper, "except I'm sure he won't tell us what they are."

"Maybe he'll share more when he gets to know us," Skunk Girl whispers. "I say we give him a chance."

"I'm not letting that jerk on our team," I whisper.

"Well, here's an idea," Selfie whispers. "What if we give him a trial period?"

"You mean, like, take him to court?" Pinball whispers.

"No, I mean that we take him on as a temporary member," Selfie whispers. "We can give him a few weeks to see how he does, and if things go well then we'll officially let him join our team."

"That's a great idea," Night Owl whispers.

"Yeah," Skunk Girl whispers, "I'll be his buddy. You know, like at school where the new kids always get a buddy to help them transition."

"Fine," Pinball whispers. "But he had better be nice."

"What do you think, Epic?" Selfie asks.

Gee, what can I say? Despite my objections, they all think this is a terrific idea. So, if I'm going to be a great leader, I guess I need to listen to my team. Even if I don't always agree.

"Fine," I whisper through gritted teeth. "But only for a trial period and then we'll see."

"Yes!" Skunk Girl says, pumping her fist.

We break and I turn to Kid Supreme. "Okay, we'll let you join Next Gen for a two-week trial period. If things go well, then we'll consider letting you join the team. But remember, that's only if things go well."

"Great," Kid Supreme says. "You won't be sorry. I won't let you down."

"We'll be the judge of that," I say.

Just then, the elevator opens and Grace steps off.

"Oh," she says, startled to see us. "I was just grabbing a jelly doughnut from the kitchen."

"Well, hey there," Kid Supreme says, his eyes lighting up as Grace walks past.

"Hmmph," Skunk Girl mutters as she crosses her arms. "What am I, chopped liver?"

"And who are you?" Grace asks, looking at Kid Supreme with disgust on her face. "Hey, aren't you that kid who took down Computron?"

"Yep, I'm Kid Supreme," he says, his biceps twitching. "I'm the newest member of Next Gen."

"Trial member," I add.

"Seriously?" Grace says, turning to me. "I was joking when I said you should get him on your team. I didn't actually expect you to add more runts for me to babysit!"

Meta Profile

Supersize

Name: Emily Shin	Height: 5'7"
Race: Human	Weight: 120 lbs
Status: Hero/Active	Eyes/Hair: Brown/Black

META 2: Meta-morph
Considerable Growth Ability
Can grow to a maximum height of 100 feet

Observed Characteristics			
Combat 58			
Durability	46	Leadership	61
Strategy	60	Willpower	82

EIGHT

I PICK UP AN UNWANTED PASSENGER

It's been a loooooong day.

I lean against my bathroom sink and stare at myself in the mirror. Based on the circles under my eyes, it looks like I've aged ten years in a single day. I can't believe how quickly things have changed.

First, there's Harmony. My alarm bells were ringing from the moment I saw her. Yet, I feel like I'm the only one who is suspicious of her intentions. After seeing what she did to Alligazer, well, that made it clear to me how dangerous she really is. Especially after she put me on notice that it was her way or the highway.

Then, there's Kid Supreme. The last thing I wanted was to give him a trial run. I mean, I can't stand the guy! But what could I do? If I'm going to be a leader then I have to respect the opinions of my team. So, now he's bunking down the hall in one of our dorm rooms. I hope the size of his ego isn't an indication of how loud he snores.

Selfie and the others went home right after we made Kid Supreme a temporary member. Unlike me, they still have regular lives to maintain. But apparently, Kid Supreme doesn't have that problem, so he asked if he could stay over and I was too tired to object.

Luckily, the bathroom has everything I need to wash up, including a toothbrush. I have to hand it to TechnocRat, he really set this place up. Of course, I do have a running punch list of improvements for him, mostly relating to AVA's glitches, but overall it's been great. I flick off the light and head to bed when I find an intruder curled up on my mattress.

"Move over, Dog-Gone," I say as I take off my boots, mask, and cape. "You know, I debated if I should let you into my room in the first place and this is how you repay me?"

Dog-Gone raises an ear but doesn't budge.

"Fine, have it your way," I say, squeezing in next to him, "but if I'm cranky tomorrow and forget to give you treats, it's your own fault."

I see the gears spinning in his head. Then, he shuffles over. Well, look at that. I guess Harmony isn't the only one with the ability to influence—at least over dogs.

"Thanks," I say. "Now get your butt off my pillow."

He shoots me a look and shimmies down.

There. Now I can finally get some—

KNOCK! KNOCK!

Seriously? What does Kid Supreme want now? I sigh, roll out of bed, and flick on the lights.

KNOCK! KNOCK!

"Hold your horses," I say as I scramble to put back on everything I just took off. I mean, the last thing I want Kid Supreme to think is that I ever slack off. "Just a minute!" I call out as I check myself in the mirror and adjust my mask. There, now I'm ready. I approach the door, puff out my chest, and throw it open, only to find—

"Took you long enough, goober," Grace says, sauntering past me into my room.

"I thought you were Kid Supreme," I say, closing the door behind her.

"Do I look like Kid Supreme?" she asks as she sits in my desk chair.

"No," I say, annoyed that I got dressed again. "Well, what do you want anyway? Is it Mom and Dad? Are they okay?"

"They're fine," she says. "Well, I hope they're fine. I haven't heard from them but that doesn't mean anything is wrong. But no, I'm here for another reason. Harmony."

"Harmony?" I say, sitting on my bed.

"Yes, Harmony," Grace says. "I've been digging around and I can't find out anything about her either."

"I told you that already," I say.

"Yeah," she says with a big smile, "but the thing is, you're not as smart as me."

"Hold on, I'm confused," I say. "Are you saying you did find out something about her? Because you just told me you didn't."

"Oh, I found something alright," she says, looking like the cat who swallowed the canary. But then she stops talking.

"Okay, I'll play along," I say, frustrated that she's dragging this out. "What did you find?"

"I'll tell you," she says, "but only after you admit that I'm smarter than you."

"You're not smarter than me," I say.

"But I am," she says. "So much smarter."

"You're not," I say.

"Fine," she says, standing up. "Sleep well."

"Okay, wait!" I say. Then, I swallow my pride and mutter, "You're smarter than me."

"Sorry, what was that?" she asks, cupping her ear. "I didn't hear you."

"You're smarter than me," I say a little louder.

"Are your fingers crossed?" she asks. "Let me see your fingers."

"Fine," I say, uncrossing my fingers. "You're smarter than me. There, are you satisfied?"

"What about your toes?"

"Come on!" I yell, frustrated.

"Okay, chill. I'll tell you," she says, sitting back down. "I couldn't find anything about Harmony, but I did find out something about that amulet she always wears around her neck."

The amulet? The eye amulet! Ugh, why didn't I think of that? I was so focused on Harmony that I didn't even think about researching her amulet.

"What about it?" I ask.

"Well, it's actually kind of interesting," Grace says. "You know TechnocRat's Infrascanner up on the Waystation?"

"Yeah," I say, "it can scan the composition of any object from a distance and tell you what it's made of."

"Right," she says, crossing her legs. "Well, while Harmony was giving a live interview on TV, I had the Infrascanner take a reading of her amulet. Guess what it found?"

"Can we stop the guessing game?" I ask. "Just tell me what it found."

"But it's fun watching you squirm," she says.

"Grace!" I bark.

"Okay, okay," she says. "It had a cosmic signature."

"Cosmic?" I say. "You mean, like, from the stars?"

"Well, kind of," she says. "Most of the reading was similar to the composition of a star, but it also had elements the Infrascanner couldn't identify. Honestly, I didn't even know that was possible. So, logically, I tried to find a match in outer space but got nothing. Then, on a whim, I figured, hey, the amulet is here on Earth so maybe there's a match somewhere on Earth. And I found one."

"You did?" I say as chills run down my spine. "From where?"

"Wanna guess?" she asks with an ear-to-ear grin.

"Grace, enough already," I say

"Party pooper," she says. "Fine. Rome."

"Rome?" I say. "As in, Rome, Italy?"

"That's the place," she says.

That's weird. The amulet is cosmic in nature, yet there's a match in Rome? Then, I remember something.

"Hey," I say. "Doesn't TechnocRat have a portable version of his Infrascanner? I think he calls it an—"

"—Infradetector?" she says. Then, she pulls out a metallic, fork-like object from her cape and says, "Here it is. I popped up to the Waystation to grab it. I already programmed in the amulet's signature so it should lead you right to the match. I wish I could check it out myself, but I'm stuck here until Mom and Dad get back."

"Thanks," I say, taking it from her. "Now I need the coordinates for where you found the match in Rome."

"Oh, I'll be happy to send them to you," she says. "Right after you tell me who's smarter again."

***

Well, that was irritating.

I do have to give Grace credit though. Researching Harmony's amulet was a genius idea. Unfortunately, I did have to tell her she was smarter than me again to get the coordinates. Of course, my toes were crossed the whole time.

And speaking of toes, as I race to the cargo elevator I hear multiple toes echoing in the hallway behind me. When I reach the elevator, I turn around to face my canine stalker.

"No, Dog-Gone," I say. "You're not coming with me. I'm going solo."

His tail stops wagging and he furrows his brow.

"You can be mad all you want," I say, "but a lot is riding on this mission and I can't risk having you screw it up when you get distracted. And trust me, you get distracted a lot."

Dog-Gone whimpers.

"Sorry, buddy," I say, stepping into the elevator. "I'll see you when I get back. AVA, take me to the Hangar."

"Certainly, Epic Zero," AVA says.

I wave goodbye to Dog-Gone and the doors close. As the elevator ascends, I feel guilty. I mean, his invisibility power could come in handy, but unfortunately, I can't manage everything else that comes with it right now. I have to get to Rome.

When the elevator reaches the fifth floor, the doors open and I'm startled to see someone wearing a black cape hunched over a computer terminal.

"Kid Supreme?" I say. "I thought you went to bed. What are you doing here?"

"Oh, hey," he says casually. "I don't sleep much so I decided to watch the news, but the reception on the Rec Room monitors is horrible. AVA wasn't responding so I thought I'd try to fix it myself. I think I traced the satellite controls to this terminal."

Hmm, AVA is clearly on the fritz, but how did he figure out the satellite controls were up here?

"So, now you know why I'm here," he says. "How about you?"

"I'm, um, going on a mission," I say, regretting the words as soon as they leave my mouth.

"A mission?" he says, his left eyebrow perking up. "Now that sounds interesting. Need a companion?"

My instincts tell me to say, 'no way,' especially after what I told Dog-Gone. But the thought of Kid Supreme wandering around the Beacon unsupervised gives me an even worse feeling. I'd better keep an eye on him.

"Um, sure," I say.

"Awesome," he says. "Where to?"

"Rome," I say. "I'll fill you in on the Gen-Jet."

"The Gen-Jet?" he says, looking at the vehicle. Then, he turns to me and flashes his mega-watt smile. "That's right, I forgot you can't fly."

"That's not true," I say, feeling annoyed. "I can fly sometimes. In fact, if you happen to make it through the trial period, which is a longshot by the way, then you'll see me do all sorts of amazing things."

"Really?" he says with surprise. "Well, I can't wait to see that. Oh, and don't worry. I'll make it through the trial period with flying colors."

I pop the hatch, and as Kid Supreme brushes past me to board the Gen-Jet, it takes everything in my power to hold my tongue.

Meta Profile

Copycat

▯ Name: Jayden Baxter	▯ Height: 5'5"
▯ Race: Human	▯ Weight: 142 lbs
▯ Status: Hero/Active	▯ Eyes/Hair: Brown/Black

META 2: Meta-morph
▯ Considerable Body Duplication
▯ Can generate unlimited identical copies of himself

Observed Characteristics			
Combat 46			
Durability	13	Leadership	60
Strategy	58	Willpower	85

NINE

I RUIN SOME RUINS

So much for going solo.

I wanted to make this trip to Rome alone, but clearly that wasn't in the cards. Especially after I found Kid Supreme wandering around the Beacon unsupervised. Believe me, the last thing I wanted to do was bring him along, but I didn't have a choice.

So, now I've got unwanted company.

Yay me.

I bristle as he kicks his boots up on the Gen-Jet's dashboard. Man, everything this kid does gets on my nerves. Sure, he's big, handsome, and powerful, but so am I. Well, at least I'm powerful.

Why does he get under my skin?

"I bet you're glad you ran into me," Kid Supreme

says, putting his hands behind his head.

Oh yeah, that's right—his obnoxious personality!

"Don't worry," he continues, "I'll manage anything that comes our way. If you were impressed by how easily I handled Computron, you should have seen me crush bad guys like Radius and Smashmouth."

"Good for you," I mutter. I have to admit, those are some impressive Meta 3 villains, but there's no way I'm telling him that!

"Of course, if we run into trouble, I can hold back a little if you want," he says. "You know, so you can show me those amazing powers you've been talking about. That is, if you actually have powers."

"For the millionth time, I have powers," I say, trying to control my temper. "They're amazing powers and I'm more than capable of dealing with any trouble, even without you here."

"Sure, sure, of course," he says dismissively. "I'm looking forward to seeing them. Hopefully."

I take a deep breath and exhale. Right now I should be focused on Harmony's eye amulet, but instead, all I can think about is how to get rid of this jerk. I scan the dashboard to see if TechnocRat installed an eject button.

"So, what's the story with Selfie?" he asks casually. "She seems cool."

Selfie? I knew it! He wouldn't be asking me about her unless he liked her. Well, I need to put a stop to that.

"Yeah, she's cool," I say. "When she's not raging."

"Raging?" Kid Supreme says surprised.

"Yeah," I say matter-of-factly. "Trust me, she's as cool as a cucumber one minute, and the next, she'll go bananas. You know, tantrums, outbursts, that kind of thing. Sometimes, she'll erupt like a volcano over nothing."

"Really?" Kid Supreme says. "I never imagined her doing that."

"Yeah, take it from me," I say, "don't get too close."

"Well, you seem tight with her," he says.

"I have to be," I say quickly. "After all, I'm the leader. It's my job to build relationships with everyone on the team, no matter how difficult they might be. That's what leaders do."

"Yeah," Kid Supreme says, scratching his chin. "I guess that's true."

"Absolutely," I say.

I glance over and see him lost in thought. Good, hopefully that worked. I feel kind of bad misrepresenting Selfie like that, but the last thing I need is for him to take a liking to her. Or even worse, her to him. Now, where is that eject button anyway?

"Destination reached," the Gen-Jet announces.

I look up to see the sun rising over Rome. No wonder it's called 'the Eternal City.' It's breathtakingly beautiful. Ancient structures are interspersed with modern buildings, creating a fascinating mix of old and new. And when you add in the cobblestone streets, rolling hills, and green parks, it's truly a magical place.

Unfortunately, we didn't come all this way to sightsee. We've got a job to do. We need to find the matching signature to Harmony's amulet.

BEEP! BEEP!

"What's that?" Kid Supreme asks, sitting up.

"A message from Glory Girl," I say, looking at the console. Great, she must be sending the coordinates she promised. Well, she certainly took her sweet time. I mean, we're already here! I click open her message, which reads:

Hey Goober Face,
Here are the coordinates:
41.8986° N, 12.4768° E
Sincerely,
The Smarter One

P.S. and you know it! ☺

She doesn't stop, does she?

I punch the coordinates into the mapping system, and up pops the following:

THE PANTHEON
AKA "THE TEMPLE OF THE GODS"

"The Pantheon?" Kid Supreme says. "Wow, that place is famous."

"Yeah, I think I've heard of it," I say as I look up its

profile. The monitor spits back:

THE PANTHEON IS A TEMPLE DEDICATED TO THE ANCIENT GODS OF ROME. BUILT BETWEEN A.D. 118 AND 125, THE PANTHEON IS THE BEST-PRESERVED ANCIENT BUILDING IN THE CITY. REMARKABLY, IT IS STILL BEING USED AS A CHURCH TO THIS DAY.

That's strange. Why is an amulet with cosmic origins connected to an ancient temple like the Pantheon?

As I lower the Gen-Jet over the city, Kid Supreme blurts out—

"Whoa, look at all of those banners."

Banners? I look down, and to my surprise, the entire city of Rome is decorated with banners featuring Harmony. It's like it's National Harmony Day or something. I can't understand what the banners say because they're all in Italian, but her smiling face is plastered everywhere.

I hadn't really thought about her impact internationally. But now that I'm seeing it in person, she's become a global icon!

"Let me see," Kid Supreme says, peering through the windshield. "They're calling Harmony the 'Greatest Humanitarian of All Time.' And some of the banners are even calling her 'The Savior.'"

"Really?" I say. "Wait, you can read Italian?"

"Yep," he says. "I know lots of languages."

Hmmm, the plot thickens.

Truthfully, I've been avoiding talking to him on this trip, but, as the team leader, I suppose I should get to know him better. I'm about to start asking questions, when—

"Destination reached," the Gen-Jet announces.

"Look," Kid Supreme says, pointing straight ahead. "That's the Pantheon."

Suddenly, I see an incredible, ancient temple situated in the middle of the city. The front entranceway has a triangular pediment supported by huge, granite columns. And behind that is an absolutely massive building, half a football field wide, with a domed roof.

But the spectacular architecture isn't the only thing I notice, because there's also a squadron of armed guards surrounding the place. It won't be easy to get inside.

Now I regret leaving Dog-Gone behind.

"I'll take care of the guards," Kid Supreme says, unbuckling his seatbelt.

"No," I say as we glide over the domed roof. "We don't want to attract any attention. Besides, I see another way in."

"Where?" he asks.

"There," I say, pointing to a large, circular hole in the center of the Pantheon's domed roof. I scroll through the Pantheon's profile. "It says it's called an oculus. The ancient Romans didn't have electricity so that hole let light into the building. I'll set the Gen-Jet on hover and we can get out and fly right through it."

"Fly?" he says. "Are you sure you can do that?"

"Don't worry," I say with a wink. "You'll see." Then, I put the Gen-Jet on hover-mode, unbuckle my seatbelt, and pop the hatch. "After you."

"Suit yourself," Kid Supreme says, and then he takes off into the air.

I concentrate, push out my duplication power, and grab his flight power. But when I pull it back in I get a strange sensation. He's powerful, that's for sure. However, there's something else about his Meta energy, something I can't quite put my finger on. But I guess I'll have to figure it out later because he's already at the domed roof.

"Wait for me," I call out as I take to the air.

He hovers above the oculus until I catch up.

"Not bad," he says, his left eyebrow rising.

"Trust me," I say, "this is just the tip of the iceberg." Then, I pull the Infradetector out of my utility belt.

"What's with the fork?" he asks.

"It's not a fork," I say. "It's an instrument that has a reading of Harmony's amulet. If there's a match here, it should lead us right to it. Now remember, this place is thousands of years old. Try not to break anything."

"Who me?" he says innocently.

We fly through the oculus into the building which, fortunately, is empty at this early hour. As I look around I feel the history of the place. The walls are lined with Renaissance-era paintings, elaborate columns, and larger-than-life statues. The marble floors are decorated with circles and squares in reds, yellows, and browns that tie into the color-scheme of the walls. It's awe-inspiring!

I take a spin around the perimeter but all the Infradetector is giving me is a dull, red light. Hmm, nothing yet. I wave the Infradetector over the statues, paintings, and columns but it doesn't pick up anything either.

Is Grace playing a practical joke on me? I wouldn't put it past her. I'm about to tell Kid Supreme we've been had when I notice he's standing in the center of the room looking straight up at the oculus.

"What are you doing?" I ask.

"Well, we're investigating Harmony's eye amulet, right?" he says. "And you said the opening in the domed roof is called an oculus."

"Yeah," I say. "So?"

"So," he says, "the word for oculus in Italian is 'oculo,' which is another word for eye, get it? We're looking for an eye inside a building that literally has a feature called an eye. That's no coincidence, is it?"

"Maybe not," I say. "But the Infradetector isn't—"

MEEP!

That's the Infradetector! And it's blinking green!

Kid Supreme was right! There must be something here. But when I look down, all I see is a small drain in the marble floor. I lower the Infradetector over the drain.

MEEP! MEEP!

"It's picking up a signal right here," I say. "Right where you're standing."

Then, Kid Supreme looks down and says, "Bingo."

"Bingo?" I say. "Bingo what?"

"There's a drainage system that goes under the floor," Kid Supreme says. "Right under the center of the oculus. It must be here to catch the rain that comes in through the opening. It runs deep."

"How do you know that?" I ask.

"Because I can see through things," he says, looking up at me. "I have X-ray vision."

X-ray vision?! Suddenly, everything makes sense.

"So, that's how you knew we were inside the Beacon," I say. "You used X-ray vision."

"Yep," he says with a shrug. "It comes in handy."

Well, isn't he just full of surprises? Suddenly, I wonder what else he can do. We're going to have a long talk after this.

"If we're going to follow that signal," he says, stepping to the side, "then we have to go down there."

"Right," I say. "Well, this is a pretty historic temple, so how do you propose we do that without damaging—"

FAZAAM!

I shield my eyes as a bright stream of red light blasts from Kid Supreme's eyes. And before I can object, he's cut a circular hole right through the marble floor!

"Are you crazy?!" I say. "Didn't you hear what I said? This place is thousands of years old!"

"I heard you," he says, stomping down on the edge of the marble cut-out, making it flip up into his hand. "But the way I see it, we've got questions and this place has answers."

Then, he lays the marble circle next to the hole, jumps inside, and disappears.

I rub my hands over my face. I can't believe it. He just wrecked a piece of irreplaceable history. I look into the black hole and don't see the bottom.

"Yo!" he calls out, his voice echoing up through the drain. "Are you coming or what?"

MEEP! MEEP! MEEP!

The Infradetector is blinking more frequently. Great, whatever we're after is clearly down this drain. If I've said it once, I've said it a million times, NOTHING GOOD EVER happens underground. But if I'm going to solve the mystery of Harmony's amulet, then that's exactly where I need to go.

So I take a deep breath, exhale, and jump into the hole.

Meta Profile

Thermo

UPDATED

Name: Lyle McGann	Height: 5'5"
Race: Human	Weight: 127 lbs
Status: Hero/Active	Eyes/Hair: Blue/Red

META 2: Energy Manipulator
Considerable Temperature Control
Can use his powers anywhere

Observed Characteristics			
Combat 40			
Durability	15	Leadership	51
Strategy	49	Willpower	53

TEN

I SEE EYE TO EYE

I'm underground… again.

I don't know why I keep ending up in these subterranean situations, but for some reason I always do. Despite how much I hate being below ground level, I had no choice but to follow Kid Supreme into the drainage system beneath the Pantheon. The Infradetector reading was pretty clear that the signal matching Harmony's eye amulet is somewhere down here. Plus, I couldn't let Kid Supreme get all the credit.

Yeah, I know how it sounds but I can't lie. The thought of Kid Supreme telling Selfie all about his daring adventure while I sat on the sidelines provided a lot of motivation. Besides, this was my mission first, so I'm going to see it through.

The drainage system below the Pantheon is dark and twisty. Even though I have my flashlight from my utility belt, I've never flown down a pipe before and I keep banging into the sides. Fortunately, the Infradetector is still blinking green and MEEPING away so we must be close to something. I just don't know what.

Suddenly, the drain lets out into a chamber. I land on my feet and point my flashlight at Kid Supreme's smirking face.

"Took you long enough," he says. "Clearly, night vision isn't one of your 'amazing' powers."

I ignore him and shine my flashlight around to get my bearings. We're inside a large, rocky cavern that must be man-made. The walls are gently curved and the ceiling is way too smooth to be natural. I notice the floor slopes down and into a small tunnel. I guess that's where the rain water goes after it exits the drain.

Okay, it's time to get down to business. I hold out the Infradetector and wave it around.

MEEP!

"What are you doing?" he asks.

"Trying to pick up the matching signal to Harmony's amulet," I say. "That's why we're down here, remember?"

MEEP! MEEP!

The Infradetector's green light starts blinking like mad. "Got it!" I say. "It's straight ahead."

"I should probably lead," Kid Supreme says. "Just in case there's something you can't handle."

Before I can respond, Kid Supreme steps in front of me and starts walking.

"Whatever," I mutter, rolling my eyes.

As we press on, the walls of the cavern start to narrow and we find ourselves walking down a tight corridor. The farther we go, the colder it gets, and my teeth start chattering.

"Hey, don't be scared," Kid Supreme says. "I'll protect you."

"I'm not scared," I say annoyed. "I'm freezing."

"Uh-huh," Kid Supreme says.

I have an overwhelming desire to clobber him from behind and leave his unconscious body down here, but I resist the temptation. I just need to get this mission over with and then I'll never have to team up with him again. At least, I hope not.

"Hold on," Kid Supreme whispers as he stops at a rock archway at the end of the corridor. "We've found another room."

I stand on my tippytoes to peer over his broad shoulders. He's right. We've reached the entrance of another cavern.

MEEP! MEEP! MEEP!

The Infradetector is going wild!

"Can you shut the volume off?" Kid Supreme asks. "It's annoying."

Not as annoying as you, I think to myself.

"No," I say. "Can you see anything in there?"

"I'll take a look," he says, peering inside. And then—

FAZAAM!

Kid Supreme startles me as he looks up and fires a blast of Heat Vision at the ceiling. Suddenly, a stalactite comes CRASHING down!

"What are you doing?!" I ask.

"That guy was coming right at us," Kid Supreme says. "Look."

But when I shine my flashlight inside the cavern, I realize that 'guy' is actually a statue. And remarkably, it's still standing despite getting slammed by Kid Supreme's stalactite.

"Night vision, huh?" I say, holding in my laughter.

"Anyone could have made that mistake," he says, crossing his arms. "He looked like a real person."

"Uh-huh," I say, mimicking the mocking tone he used on me.

I step over the rubble to examine the marble statue. As I run my flashlight over it, I have to admit that Kid Supreme was right. It really does look like an actual person. The level of detail put into the man's facial features and toga is extraordinary. Then, I notice the statue is holding a coin in the outstretched palm of his right hand. There are also a bunch of symbols etched into the marble base he's standing on, but I have no idea what they mean.

"It says, 'Sors, the God of Luck,'" Kid Supreme says.

"Wait, you can read that?" I ask.

"Sure," he says. "I told you I'm good with languages. The ancient Romans spoke classical Latin."

Wow. I mean, Italian is one thing but he knows classical Latin too? That's pretty astounding, but what's even more astounding is this statue.

What's it doing beneath the Pantheon?

Then, I look to my left and gasp, because there's a foot! I quickly shine my flashlight and realize the foot belongs to another statue. And there are dozens more against the wall! It feels like we're inside a museum, except we're not.

"This statue is of 'Muta, the Goddess of Silence,'" Kid Supreme says.

"That's funny, I didn't even know there was a Goddess of Silence," I say, thinking of how helpful she would be in dealing with Grace.

"Yeah," Kid Supreme says. "The Romans had all kinds of minor Gods. This one is 'Lactans, the God of Agriculture.' Back then they worshipped a different God or Goddess for every aspect of their life."

"That's great," I say. "But why are they down here?"

MEEP! MEEP! MEEP! MEEP!

Okay, now the Infradetector is really going nuts. We keep walking as Kid Supreme translates the names of the other statues, like 'Cardea, the Goddess of Thresholds and Door Hinges,' and 'Fornax, the Goddess of Bread Baking and Ovens.' The Infradetector still hasn't made a match but Kid Supreme was right—the Romans had a deity for everything. I wonder if there's a 'God of Stopping German Shepherds from Snoring.'

We keep going until I see a statue of a woman that's different. All of the other statues are standing, but this one is kneeling.

MOOOOP! MOOOOP!

Moop? The Infradetector is making a new noise, and the light isn't blinking anymore, it's solid green!

This has to be it!

I lean over to look at the statue's face and gasp! Her left eye, it's… gone! I mean, there's an actual gap where her eye should be! It's like someone dug it out!

"Hey, Kid Supreme, over here!" I call out. "Hurry! What does this statue say?"

"Let's see," he says, kneeling. "It says, 'Suadela, the Goddess of Persuasion.'"

Persuasion? The hairs on the back of my neck stand on end, and suddenly everything clicks! The Infradetector just matched the reading from Harmony's eye amulet with the statue of Suadela, the Goddess of Persuasion! Which means the eye in Harmony's eye amulet must be the missing eye from Suadela's statue!

But… she's just a statue. Right?

Then, I remember what Grace said about the Infrascanner's initial reading. She said the Infrascanner identified Harmony's amulet as cosmic in nature, but with other elements it couldn't identify. If the eye amulet was made of marble then it would have been easy to identify.

But it wasn't.

I touch Suadela's cold, solid arm. She looks like a statue and feels like a statue, yet according to the Infrascanner, she's not a statue at all.

So, does that means she was once…

O. M. G!

"So, are you thinking what I'm thinking?" Kid Supreme asks.

"Um, that depends," I say, swallowing hard. "What are you thinking?"

"I'm thinking that Harmony came down here and took the eye from this statue," he says. "And somehow, through magic or something else, she's using it to get everyone to do what she wants."

"Um, yeah," I say, "that's what I'm thinking too." I mean, at least that's partly what I'm thinking. But I don't want to tell him the other half of what's going through my head. Because if my theory is correct, then this statue of Suadela wasn't always just a statue—she was once alive!

I look at all of the other statues and my jaw drops. If Suadela had been alive, then that means all of these other statues were alive once too! Which means that actual Gods and Goddesses walked on Earth! But now, for some reason, they're all statues.

"Hey, what's this?" Kid Supreme says, examining the wall behind Suadela. "That doesn't look natural."

I raise my flashlight and realize he's right. While the

rest of the cavern has solid walls, the area behind Suadela is covered in large, stacked rocks. It looks like a doorway!

"Stand back," Kid Supreme says, rearing back his fist, and then—POW!

I shield my face as he punches through the wall, and when I look back up he's opened an entranceway into an entirely new cavern!

"Come on," Kid Supreme says.

I step over the debris and follow him inside. It's just as dark in this part of the cavern, and when I shine my flashlight I do a double take because we're standing before a group of ten statues that are neatly arranged in a semi-circle.

I scan the largest statue with my flashlight. This one is a muscular, older man with serious eyes and a long, flowing beard. He's wearing a crown and holding a long scepter in his left hand.

"That's Jupiter," Kid Supreme says. "'The God of Thunder and Lightning.'"

"Jupiter?" I say.

"Yep," Kid Supreme says. "He's the ruler of all the Gods. He's the Roman equivalent of the Greek god, Zeus. The minor Gods were all outside, but this chamber is holding the major Roman Gods. There are supposed to be thirteen of them, but three seem to be missing. I can read you the ones who are here. Look, we've got 'Apollo, the God of Music;' 'Ceres, the Goddess of the Harvest;' 'Diana, the Goddess of the Hunt;' 'Juno, Queen of the

Gods and the Goddess of Fertility;' 'Mercury, the God of Travelers and Tradesmen;' 'Neptune, the God of the Sea;' 'Pluto, the God of the Underworld,' 'Vesta, the Goddess of Hearth and Home;' and 'Vulcan, the God of Blacksmiths and Volcanoes.' That's ten including Jupiter."

"Which ones are missing?" I ask.

"Well," Kid Supreme says, "I don't see statues for Mars, the God of War, or Minerva, the Goddess of Wisdom, or Venus, the Goddess of Love. I wonder where those statues are?"

Now there's a great question.

"Anyway, I wonder why these statues are down here," Kid Supreme says. "You'd think they'd be on display inside the Pantheon, not under it, right?"

"Yeah," I say, my mind spinning.

BEEP! BEEP! BEEP!

Huh? I look down at the Infradetector but it's not making noise. Then I realize the beeping is coming from the Freedom Force transmitter in my belt. I push the button and say, "Hello?"

"–in Goober Face, do you read me?" comes Grace's voice.

Grace? What does she want?

"Yes, Glory Girl," I say. "I read you. What's up?"

"Well, first your dog hasn't stopped whining since you left him here," she says. "I gave him a boatload of doggie treats to shut him up, but it didn't work. And now

I think he barfed on your pillow."

"Um, gee, thanks," I say, rolling my eyes. "Is that really why you're calling me right now?"

"No, there's something I thought you should know," she says. "Your entire team just quit Next Gen to join the Game Changers."

"What?!" I exclaim. "A-Are you joking?"

"I wish," she says. "I was just in the kitchen and saw that Selfie left you a note. It was right on the refrigerator door so I read it, sorry. Anyhoo, I thought you should know. I've gotta split now in case I hear from Mom and Dad. Later."

CLICK!

I'm stunned.

Selfie and the others just quit Next Gen.

But… why?

"Hey, are you okay?" Kid Supreme asks.

"No," I say, "not really."

ELEVEN

I AM A TEAM OF ONE

I'm at a loss for words.

Kid Supreme, on the other hand, is chatting up a storm on our ride back to the Beacon. I pretend to listen, but all I can think about is Grace's news. My entire team just quit to join Harmony and the Game Changers. And they didn't even have the courtesy to tell me in person!

Yet, after what we found in Rome, I'm not sure they left of their own free will. That's because we discovered that the eye in Harmony's amulet came from the statue of Suadela, the Goddess of Persuasion! And according to TechnocRat's Infrascanner, Suadela's statue is part cosmic and part unknown, which makes me think that Suadela was once alive and real Gods walked the Earth!

Now there's a mindblower for ya.

However, as crazy as that seems, all I can deal with is the here-and-now. Which means that my friends have joined up with Harmony and I'm a leader without a team. Just thinking about her makes my blood boil.

Now I know how she's making everything happen. She's using the eye of Suadela to control everyone. So, maybe she's not a Psychic after all. But if she's not, then what are her actual powers? And more importantly, why is she doing all of this in the first place?

I wish I had the answers but I don't. And that's not all that's worrying me. As much as I want to believe that Selfie and the others were brainwashed by Harmony, what if they weren't? I mean, when I think back to my argument with Selfie in the Combat Room, she seemed completely like herself. She genuinely believed in Harmony's vision for the future.

So, Harmony could have influenced my friends to join her, but what if she didn't? I swallow hard. I sure hope Selfie's note provides some answers.

"Destination reached," the Gen-Jet announces.

There's the Beacon. I punch in the commands to open the Hangar and we land a few seconds later.

"Thanks for your help," I say to Kid Supreme. "But if you don't mind, I'd like to be alone for a while."

"Oh, sure, no problem," Kid Supreme says. "I'll see if I can fix that monitor reception problem."

I nod, pop the hatch, and head for the elevator.

"AVA," I say, "please take me to the first floor."

"Certainly, Epic Zero," AVA says.

As we descend, I can't help but think of all the crazy adventures we've had as Next Gen—from our first mission fighting Erase Face to saving the world from the clutches of Krule the Conqueror. I think about all of the fun we had hanging out together at the treehouse, watching movies, and joking around. Now, I won't hear Pinball and Skunk Girl busting on each other, Night Owl's sarcastic comments, or Selfie's, well, everything.

"First floor," AVA says as the doors slide open.

I pause inside the elevator and survey the empty Rec Room. As I make my way to the kitchen, I see the note Selfie left for me pinned to the refrigerator door by a Freedom Force logoed magnet. It's folded over with the word 'EPIC' written in large, bold letters. Of course, that didn't stop Grace from reading it.

I grab the note, take a deep breath, and exhale. Then, I open it and see Selfie's neat handwriting:

Hi Epic,

We hope your mission went well. We're so sorry we couldn't be there to tell you this in person, but we didn't know when you were coming back and we couldn't wait. Anyway, we know this will be hard for you like it is for us, so you might want to sit down before you finish reading this note.

Are you sitting down? Well, here goes. While you were gone, we had a meeting and decided to accept Harmony's invitation to join the Game Changers. Please believe us when we tell you this was a difficult decision. After all, we've loved being a part of Next Gen and we are so thankful for you and our new headquarters. But we believe in Harmony's mission. She really is changing the world for the better, and we feel obligated to use our powers to help her.

Please don't take this personally. Trust me, this has nothing to do with you. We've all enjoyed having you as our leader, even Skunk Girl. You've taught us so much about teamwork and what it means to be a hero, and more importantly, how to believe in ourselves.

This is heart-wrenching for all of us, but we believe we can use our gifts to make a bigger impact in the world. Of course, this doesn't have to be the end. You can still join us! We'd love to have you fighting alongside us again—especially me. Please, think about it.

See you soon?
Selfie and the Team

I read the note again from top to bottom and crumple it in my hands. Whew, that was tough. What's worse is that it didn't sound like they were brainwashed. I mean, if they were brainwashed they wouldn't have bothered to leave a note at all!

Which basically means I've lost them for good.

I feel like a total failure. One of my dreams was to be like Dad and lead a team of great Meta heroes. I can't imagine Dad ever losing the Freedom Force.

A tear rolls down my cheek and I wipe it away.

Clearly, they liked Harmony's leadership better than mine. I guess saving the plain old universe just isn't enough anymore. I mean, was I wrong? Could I have done more? Should I have done more?

"Elliott?"

Grace's voice startles me and I turn to see her standing behind me. "What do you want?" I snap.

"Hey," she says, raising her hands. "I just wanted to see how you were doing."

"So you can make fun of me?" I ask, wiping my tears away. "Well, no thanks."

"Look, I'm not here to make fun of you," Grace says. "I'm your big sister. Believe it or not, but I actually do care about you, okay?"

I look into her eyes and more tears start streaming down my cheeks. "I-I can't believe they left."

"I'm so sorry," she says, hugging me. "Bring it in, but if you use my cape as a tissue I'm going to deck you."

I chuckle. "Thanks," I say, letting her go.

"No problem," she says. "Just don't tell Mom. After all, I do have a reputation to uphold. Look, I know the situation with your friends is hard, but I'm curious about what you learned in Rome."

Grace scratches her chin as I give her the download about Suadela. "Hmm," she says, "that is super suspicious."

"Yeah," I say. "I think it's time to expose Harmony and what she's really doing."

"You know," Grace says, "I think she's about to give a live interview right now. AVA, please put on CNC."

"Certainly, Glory Girl," AVA says. "Stand by."

CNC? That's the network where I did my televised interview with Sara Anderson and General Winch. But instead of CNC, AVA puts on a show with talking puppets.

"AVA, wrong channel," Grace says frustrated.

"Apologies, Glory Girl," AVA says. "Here is CNC."

The channel switches and I see Sara Anderson sitting across from Harmony in front of the Washington Monument. An enormous crowd has gathered to see them and they're holding signs praising Harmony.

But that's not all. The Game Changers are standing behind Harmony, including Selfie and the rest of my team!

"Harmony," Sara Anderson says, "thank you so much for carving out time for this in-depth interview. You've been such a positive force since you came on the scene and the people want to know everything about you. You've already made so many things happen it's impossible to recap them all, but maybe we can go over a few so we can get your valuable perspective?"

"I'd be happy to, Ms. Anderson," Harmony says with a big smile.

"Great," Sara Anderson says. "Let's start with Meta crime. You promised a reduction in Meta crime, and according to our statistics, Meta crimes have decreased to almost zero since just last week. That's remarkable."

"Thank you, Ms. Anderson," Harmony says. "As you can see by the collection of brave heroes standing behind us, we've increased our ranks with Metas who share our vision of bringing positive change to society. In addition, our zero-tolerance policy against criminals has been very effective. Since its implementation, many criminals have simply decided to retire instead of facing the consequences of their reprehensible actions. In addition, we've begun to decommission the prison system, including the maximum-security Meta prison known as Lockdown. This action alone will save the world millions of dollars a year. Imagine what we could do with those resources instead?"

What? Decommission Lockdown? Is she kidding?

"That is impressive," Sarah Anderson says. "Speaking of resources, you've done an amazing job working with world leaders to reallocate resources across the globe. Will you talk about that some more?"

"Absolutely," Harmony says. "I've personally met with every world leader to share my expectations about arms de-escalation, the redistribution of food, and—"

As she goes on, bragging about everything she's done, the only thing I can focus on is the eye amulet around her neck. Now that I've seen Suadela's statue, it's clear to me that it's an exact match. It's the same color, the same size…

"That's amazing," Sarah Anderson says. "You know,

this tremendous crowd has come here to see you today."

The crowd CHEERS.

"You've become a global superstar," Sara Anderson continues, "and although we've never had one person running the planet before, I understand that laws are being rewritten to make you the official leader of the entire world."

Wait, what?

"Yes, I heard," Harmony says, putting her hand over her heart. "I'm truly touched. I never thought my hopes and dreams for this planet would lead to all of this. But if this is what the people want, who am I to object?"

"Oh, she's good," Grace says, shaking her head in disapproval. "Really good."

Okay, this has gone far enough.

I turn and head for the elevator.

"Hey," Grace calls out. "Where are you going?"

"To put an end to this," I say. "Stay tuned, because I'm about to reveal Harmony's secret to the entire world."

Meta Profile

Monsoon

UPDATED

Name: Mikey Waterson	Height: 4'10"
Race: Human	Weight: 101 lbs
Status: Hero/Active	Eyes/Hair: Blue/Brown

META 2: Meta-morph

- Considerable Water Morphing
- Can turn all or parts of his body into pure water

Observed Characteristics			
Combat 38			
Durability	50	Leadership	21
Strategy	19	Willpower	36

TWELVE

I EXPOSE THE TRUTH

Everyone is about to learn the shocking truth.

Once I expose Harmony for the fraud she really is on national television, her entire house of cards will come crashing down. Everyone will realize that she's been manipulating them with the eye of Suadela. Then, the world will regain its sanity and I'll get my friends back.

I can't wait.

Fortunately, it didn't take long to reach Washington D.C. in the Gen-Jet. Harmony's interview at the Washington Monument is still going on and it's being broadcast to every station in the world. I need to get there fast so I can surprise her live on the air, but if she sees the Gen-Jet coming she'll sick the Game Changers on me and I'll never reach her.

So, instead of parking at the Washington Monument, I come in low and touch down a few blocks away in Federal Triangle. Then, I pop the hatch and start running. I head south toward the National Mall, the park-like area that connects most of the iconic buildings in Washington D.C., from the U.S. Capitol to the Lincoln Memorial. The Washington Monument is over five hundred feet tall and towers over the surrounding area.

The symbolism of this location isn't lost on me. The Washington Monument was built to honor George Washington, the first president of the United States. Clearly, Harmony wanted to be interviewed here in a not-so-subtle attempt to link herself with our country's first national hero.

Well, I'm afraid her plan is about to be interrupted.

I'm running so fast I'm going to be out of breath by the time I reach her, so I settle into a brisk walk instead. But the closer I get, the larger the crowd becomes. I can't believe how many people are here. The crowd is stretched all the way down Independence Avenue! People from all walks of life are hanging on her every word, which is blaring out of speakers placed around the National Mall. Luckily, everyone is facing the monument, which means no one will notice a costumed kid like me slipping through the crowd.

As I jostle through the sea of humanity, I try to remember if I put deodorant on this morning. But I guess that doesn't matter right now. After all, I'm not here for a social visit. Finally, I reach the sidewalk in front of the Washington Monument and take in the scene.

Police barriers surround the monument, keeping the crowd about fifty feet back. An army of police officers is standing behind the barriers, facing the crowd. Well, that's not helpful. Somehow, I'll need to get past them to reach Harmony, who is sitting with Sara Anderson on the paved, circular pathway at the base of the monument itself.

Harmony may be far away, but I can see her grinning from ear to ear. Boy, I can't wait to wipe that smile off her face. I take note of the cameras, the news crews, and the row of Metas standing behind her. There are the usual suspects, like Thermo, Monsoon, Supersize, and Copycat. But alongside them are Pinball, Night Owl, Skunk Girl, and Selfie!

Anger wells up inside of me when I see my friends—my team—backing Harmony. I still can't believe they left me for her.

"Yes, I would work hard to be a good and fair world leader," I hear Harmony say. "I'll always keep the interests of the people above my own."

Suddenly, the crowd starts chanting, "HARMONY! HARMONY! HARMONY!"

Okay, I've officially heard enough. I see lights on the TV cameras, which means we're still live. Now's the time to make my move!

I concentrate hard and copy Night Owl's Meta

energy. Then, I create a shadow slide and ride it right over the heads of the stunned police officers.

"Sorry to interrupt this broadcast," I say, dropping in front of Sarah Anderson and Harmony, "but I've got a newsflash of my own!"

This is it! My big moment. I open my mouth, ready to unveil the truth to billions of people, when—

"Hey, I know you!" Sarah Anderson exclaims. "You're Epic Zebra!"

I feel my shoulders sag. Well, that wasn't quite the start I was hoping for. Suddenly, the cops pull their guns and Supersize grows a hundred feet tall!

"I'll clobber him!" Supersize says, raising her fist.

Uh-oh.

"No! Everyone freeze!" Harmony commands as she raises her hand high into the air. Then, she looks at me with an amused expression and says, "He clearly wanted to make a dramatic entrance, and I'm curious to hear what he has to say."

"Oh, I've got plenty to say," I shoot back, regaining my mojo. Then, I point to her amulet and say, "Like, you're a phony! I went to Rome and I know that eye you're wearing around your neck is from Suadela, the Goddess of Persuasion! Somehow, you're using it to brainwash everyone into doing exactly what you want and now they know it too!"

There, I did it! I put my hands on my hips and look proudly at the crowd, expecting cheers, applause, or to be showered with roses. But to my surprise, no one is moving!

Supersize's clenched fist is still raised in the air, the cops still have their weapons drawn, and Sarah Anderson is still smiling at me. What's going on? Why aren't they doing anything?

Then, it hits me. Harmony told everyone to 'freeze,' which means they're literally frozen! And what's worse is they probably didn't hear a word I just said! Then, I look at the TV cameras and the lights are off, which means the broadcast was stopped. So, no one watching from home heard me either!

"Wh-Who are you?" I ask.

"Oh, that is not the question," Harmony says coolly, rising from her seat. But what's up with her voice? It suddenly sounded deeper, more formal. "I think the real question is, who are you?"

"What do you mean?" I ask, stepping back.

"It seems that you have gone to great lengths to discredit me," she says. "And I will not deny that what you have said is true. After all, I am using Suadela's eye to get what I want. Yet, you seem to be immune to her power. Now, why would that be?"

Immune to her power? Suddenly, I realize she's right! Unlike everyone else, I've never wavered in my thinking about Harmony. But… why?

Is the negation part of my Meta Manipulation powers keeping me from falling under the eye's influence? It could be, but what about Grace? Why hasn't she fallen in with Harmony?

Then, I remember she was sleeping when Harmony introduced herself at the UN. And when Grace watched the replay she was with me! Did my Meta energy protect her from Suadela's eye as well?

Suddenly, I realize something else. When Harmony invited my team to join her we were all together. But it was only when I was away on my mission that they left me. So, maybe they didn't willingly join the Game Changers after all!

Well, if I can negate the amulet's power of persuasion for myself, then maybe I can do it for everyone else too! I concentrate hard and direct my negation energy toward Harmony's eye amulet. But when I look up nothing has changed! Selfie and the others are still frozen! I hyper-focus and extend my arms, giving it everything I've got, but it still doesn't work!

"Fool," Harmony says. "You are but a mere mortal. Only a God can destroy another God!"

A… God?!

"I have grown tired of you," she says. "You have been lucky thus far, but your luck has run out. Now the entire world will watch you die, and I will enjoy watching your friends do the job."

My friends?

"Unfreeze," Harmony commands.

Suddenly, everyone starts moving again and the lights

on the news cameras have turned back on!

"Former members of Next Gen," Harmony calls out. "Your old teammate has dared to threaten me. Show him where your loyalty lies. Show him what happens when our zero-tolerance policy is violated."

"Yes, Harmony," my friends say in unison.

Whoa! Suddenly, Selfie and the others are looking at me like I'm the worst villain of all time! I don't know what to do. I mean, these are my friends. I don't want to hurt them.

"Easy, team," I say, backing up. "Look, it's me."

But there's no warmth in their eyes.

And then they attack!

"Look into my phone, traitor!" Selfie calls out.

I shield my face before she can hypnotize me, but—

"Cowabunga, cretin!" Pinball yells.

POW!

He SLAMS into me so hard I go flying into the air, only to be caught by a black shadow net that wraps around my entire body, squeezing me tight!

"I'll take your breath away!" Night Owl shouts.

Hard to… breathe. Need to… act. I muster all the concentration I can and push out my negation power. Suddenly, the shadow net evaporates and I drop hard to the ground. Ouch, my shoulder! But as I scramble to my feet, I smell something so overwhelmingly rotten that it knocks me back down to my knees.

"What's wrong?" Skunk Girl asks. "Smell trouble?"

I try to stand up but the smell is so bad I can't think straight. I-I feel like I'm suffocating, like the foul odor is inside my brain. I… can't focus.

"Finish him off!" Selfie yells.

S-Selfie? N-No. It… it's me!

I crumple to the ground as the four of them approach. I try telling them to stop but I can't form the words. I can't believe this is how it's going to end. I can't believe my friends are going to kill—

SWOOOSH!

I'm yanked hard by my cape and suddenly I'm airborne! My friends' surprised faces shrink into the distance as I climb higher and higher into the sky.

I look up, expecting to see Grace holding onto me, but instead, it's—

"K-Kid Supreme?"

And then I pass out.

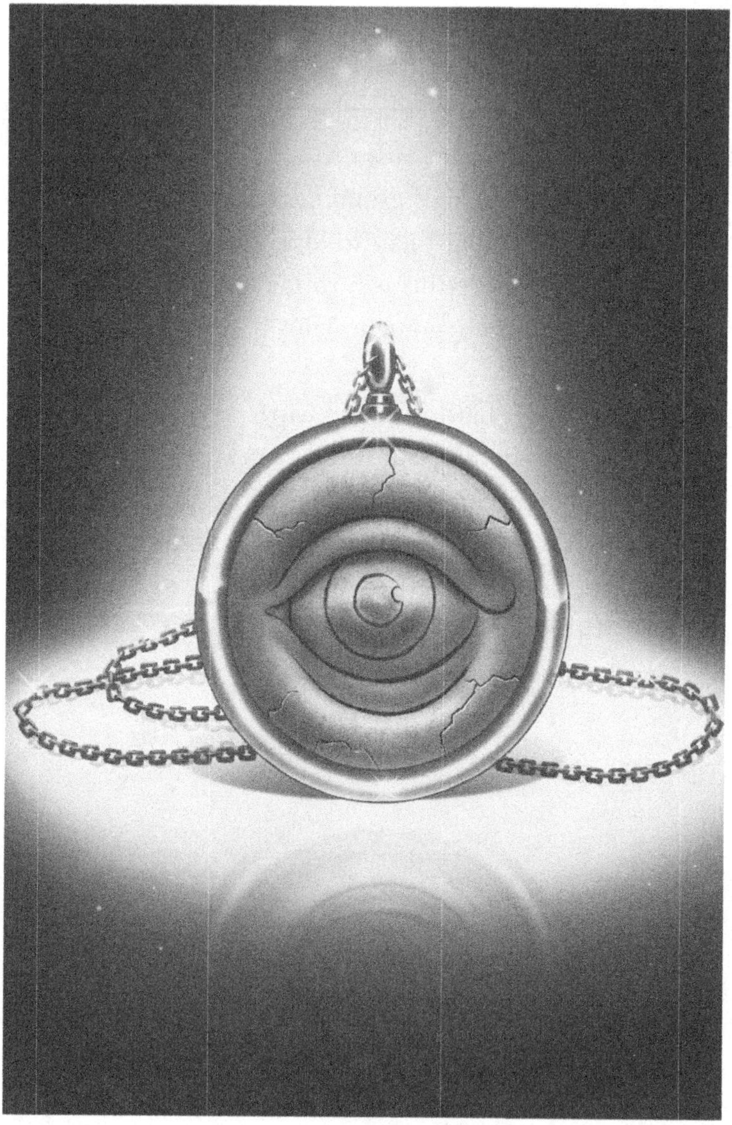

THIRTEEN

I PRESS MY LUCK

I wake with a start.

W-Where am I? I look around and notice an IV in my arm, a monitor tracking my vital signs, and a bowl of tapioca pudding on a tray by my bed. Okay, clearly I'm in the Medi-wing on the Waystation, but how did I get here? Fortunately, I don't have to wait for an answer.

"You're awake," Grace says, as she enters with Kid Supreme and Dog-Gone in tow. "Do you know how many times I kept your dog from eating your pudding?"

Dog-Gone lowers his head guiltily.

"Thanks," I say, "but I don't like tapioca pudding."

"You don't? Well, I do," she says. Then, she picks up the bowl and inhales a big spoonful as Dog-Gone watches longingly.

"What happened?" I ask, rubbing the back of my head. "I feel like I was hit by a freight train."

"You mean, you really don't remember?" Kid Supreme asks as he leans against the wall and crosses his muscular arms. "Your old teammates nearly demolished you on live TV. I kind of felt embarrassed for you actually. Luckily for you, I was there to save you. Again."

That's right! I confronted Harmony in Washington D.C. and told her she was a fraud. But I'm guessing no one heard me because she told everyone to freeze and turned off the cameras. When she was done listening to me, she set everything back to normal and ordered my friends to kill me.

"I wouldn't worry about it," he says. "Only a few billion people were watching."

A few… billion?

Just. Freaking. Wonderful.

Time to change the subject.

"So, what are we doing on the Waystation?" I ask.

"Well, we couldn't exactly go to the Beacon," Grace says between mouthfuls of tapioca. "After Kid Supreme got you out of there and recovered the Gen-Jet, Harmony sent her minions to find you. Of course, your old friends went immediately to the Beacon. Here, see for yourself."

Grace picks up the remote from the counter and flicks on the monitor. Suddenly, images appear from inside the Beacon! That's right, Mom told us they installed cameras to keep an eye on us.

But clearly, my parents aren't the only ones who want to keep tabs on me, because my friends are tearing the Beacon apart looking for me. Night Owl is flipping over the ping pong table in the Rec Room, Skunk Girl is knocking over chairs in the Mission Room, and Pinball is breaking down the door to my bedroom! Grace was right, they are after me! Then, I see Selfie in the Hangar typing into a computer.

"Don't worry, she won't be able to track us," Grace says. "I erased all records of our trip to the Waystation."

"That was smart," I say, "but Selfie knows about the Waystation. In fact, they all do. They've been here before."

"Really?" Kid Supreme says, looking out a porthole into outer space. "Well, I'd rather be up here than on Earth any day. Hey, do you think the rest of the Freedom Force will be back soon? I'd love to meet them in person."

"Unlikely," Grace says. "And don't get comfortable because you're not staying long. We normally don't allow strangers here, but this time we had no choice."

"Strangers?" Kid Supreme says. "Sheesh, that's harsh. I rescue your friend and I'm still considered a stranger, huh? Well, can I at least get a tour before you kick me out?"

"Good God no!" Grace exclaims.

Good. God?

Harmony! I hop out of bed.

"Where do you think you're going?" Grace asks. "And look out for your—"

I walk five steps and YEOW! Suddenly, I feel a sharp pain in my left arm as something pulls me back.

"—IV," she finishes.

"I'm going to the Mission Room," I say as I remove the IV and ignore Kid Supreme's laughter. Then, I gather my remaining dignity and march out of the room.

"Hey, wait up!" Grace calls out.

As they follow me down the hall we hear a loud CRASH from the Medi-Wing, which means Dog-Gone just got whatever tapioca pudding was left. Fabulous. I enter the Mission Room, sit down at the computer, and start typing away.

"What are you doing?" Kid Supreme asks.

"When I faced Harmony she called me a 'mere mortal,'" I say. "And then she said that only a God can destroy another God."

"A God?" Grace says. "She's calling herself a God now? That girl has some ego."

Well, isn't that the pot calling the kettle black? It takes everything I've got to hold my tongue, but I stay on task as the computer returns the results of my search query. Unfortunately, it says: NO RESULTS FOUND.

"What are you searching for?" Kid Supreme asks.

"I was seeing if there were any kid Gods or Goddesses in Roman mythology," I answer. "But apparently there's not so we're back to square one."

"So, wait a second," Kid Supreme says. "Are you saying that you think Harmony is actually a Goddess?"

"Maybe," I say, spinning in my chair.

"Did you hear that?" he says, turning to Grace with a big smirk on his face. "Can you believe this guy?"

"Yes, actually," she says, crossing her arms. "After all, she is wearing Suadela's eye as an amulet. You remember Suadela, don't you? The Goddess of Persuasion."

"Well, yeah," he says with a nervous smile. "I mean, of course, I remember that."

"I wonder if that's why the Meta Monitor isn't picking up her Meta signature," I say. "Maybe it can't detect Gods."

"It's possible," Grace says. "I don't think the Freedom Force has ever encountered a God before."

"I don't think so either," I say. "There's Order and Chaos, of course, but they're more like celestial beings than Gods. Plus, when I was facing her I tried to negate the power of her eye amulet but it didn't work. That's when she told me that only a God could destroy another God. So, what if she really is a God? What if 'mere mortals' like us can't stop her?"

"Speak for yourself," Kid Supreme says, slapping his big bicep. "You may have bombed but she hasn't faced me yet. When I show up, well, let's just say it'll be her unlucky day."

Unlucky day?

Suddenly, a lightbulb goes off.

I jump out of my chair and race for the door.

"Does he always do this?" Kid Supreme asks.

"Yep, it's pretty annoying too," Grace answers.

"Don't just stand there!" I call back. "Come on!"

I bolt into the hallway and leap over a lethargic Dog-Gone who is lying on his side in the middle of the floor. "It's your own fault," I say. "You know you're not supposed to eat tapioca pudding."

Dog-Gone whimpers.

I race up the stairs to the Monitor Room, hop into the leather chair, and punch in some commands. By the time Grace and Kid Supreme arrive, I've already located the Meta signature of the person I'm looking for. Except, she's not where I thought she would be.

"Who is that?" Kid Supreme asks as he looks at the Meta profile on my screen.

"Her?" I say. "She's the only chance we've got."

***

Well, the last place I thought I'd find my friend is in a psychiatric hospital. Yet, here I am. Psychiatric hospitals are where people go to be treated for severe mental illnesses. I have to say, I was pretty nervous when we first arrived. After all, movies usually depict facilities like this as scary places, with patients screaming and yelling to get out. But this hospital is nothing like that. It's clean, quiet, and cheerfully decorated.

Against my better judgment, I decided to drag a sick Dog-Gone along so I could use his invisibility power to get around undetected. And when I say 'drag' I mean it, because he's still suffering from eating the tapioca pudding on the Waystation. Even though we're both invisible, I can hear his footsteps fading further and further into the background.

"Keep up," I whisper. "You have four legs for a reason." Seconds later, he pads up beside me and presses his furry head against my glove. "Thank you. And remember how crummy you feel the next time you try to eat tapioca pudding."

As we make our way through the halls, I'm glad I made Kid Supreme stay outside in the Gen-Jet. He wasn't happy about it but subtlety is not one of his super powers. Thanks to Dog-Gone's invisibility, I was able to flip through a clipboard at the front desk that listed all of the patients and their room numbers. Now we just need to find room C-13.

Here's C-09. C-11. Bingo! C-13.

We stand outside the closed door and I take a deep breath. This is it. The one person who can help us is inside this room. But I don't know her mental state. Will she even be able to help me? I guess it's time to find out.

"Listen up, boy," I whisper to Dog-Gone, "you wait out here and warn me if anyone is coming."

Dog-Gone plops down on my foot. Great, he

doesn't look well enough to do much of anything. Okay, here goes nothing. I turn the knob, open the door, and step over Dog-Gone to go inside.

The room is tiny, about the size of a large closet, with white walls and sparse furnishings. A brown-haired girl is lying in bed holding the covers up to her startled, brown eyes. Even though she's not wearing her purple mask, I recognize her immediately. I close the door behind me and turn off Dog-Gone's invisibility power.

"Hi, Haywire," I say calmly. "It's good to see you."

"Y-You?" she says panicked. "D-Don't call me by that name." Then, she reaches for a button on her nightstand. "I-I'll call for help."

"Haywire… Hayley, wait," I say calmly. "Please, just hear me out. I'm your friend, remember? And I need your help."

Her shaky hand hovers over the button but she doesn't press it.

"Thanks," I say relieved. "Look, I-I don't want to sound insensitive, but what are you doing here?"

"I-I asked my parents to bring me here," she says. "You see, after… Siphon. Well, things just weren't the same."

That's right! The last time I saw her is when we battled Siphon at Safari Park. He hurt her pretty badly. Afterward, she said that she didn't want to be a hero anymore and I lost track of her.

"I-I mean, you know how my powers work," she

continues as tears run down her cheeks. "You know that whenever I'm around, bad things happen… dangerous things. And they've become harder and harder to control. After a while, I realized it wasn't safe for me to be around anyone, especially my parents. They could get hurt… or killed. So, I-I needed a place where I couldn't hurt anyone anymore. Where I could be alone."

I feel horrible for her. She's basically isolated herself to protect society, including her parents. But I get it. I mean, her Meta powers generate bad luck. She's completely unpredictable.

And that's why I need her.

But she seems so fragile right now.

"I'm so sorry," I say sincerely. "I-I can't even imagine what you're going through."

"Thanks," she says, grabbing a tissue to wipe the tears away. "I won't lie, every day is a challenge. They mostly leave me alone here. I get my meals dropped off and I talk to the doctors on video when it works. My parents come up now and then but I only let them stay for a few minutes. It's been weeks since their last visit. But I'm trying to control my powers. I-I really am."

"I believe you and I know you can do it," I say. "I've seen you in action. I know how brave you are. And that's why I need your help. The world needs your help."

"My help?" she says. "No, I-I can't leave here. I don't want to be a hero anymore."

"Look, I understand," I say, "but without you, I can't

stop Harmony."

"Harmony?" she says. "Who's Harmony?"

Huh? Is she joking? I mean, you'd have to be living under a rock not to know who Harmony is. Or… in a psychiatric hospital.

"So, you really don't know who Harmony is?" I ask. "You know, she's the one all over TV. She has a white costume and wears an eye amulet."

"Sorry," she says, "but we're not allowed to watch TV here. We can't even have a cell phone. I mostly just read books."

Holy cow! She really doesn't know. Which also means she's not under Harmony's influence!

"Listen," I say, sitting down on the edge of her bed, "I'm going to tell you what's been happening to everyone out in the world, including your parents. After that, I think you'll understand why I'm here. Then, you can decide if you want to help me or not."

"Okay," she says, sitting up. "But I-I know I can't fight again. I'm too dangerous."

"That's okay," I say. "If you decide to help me, I promise you won't have to fight anyone."

Meta Profile

Haywire

▯ **Name: Hayley Providence**	▯ **Height: 5'0"**
▯ **Race: Human**	▯ **Weight: 87 lbs**
▯ **Status: Hero/Active**	▯ **Eyes/Hair: Brown/Brown**

META 1: Energy Manipulator

▯ **Limited Bad Luck Generation**

▯ **Power activation will cause random acts of poor luck**

Observed Characteristics			
Combat 20			
Durability	11	Leadership	26
Strategy	19	Willpower	45

FOURTEEN

I MAKE THE ULTIMATE SACRIFICE

My team is in place.

At least, I hope my team is in place.

Now all I need is a plan.

"Well, genius, what do we do next?" Grace asks.

I wish I knew. Ever since we got back from the psychiatric hospital, I've been pacing the halls of the Waystation wondering the exact same thing. Unfortunately, there's no easy answer. Every time I've faced Harmony, I'm the one who comes out worse for wear. And I'm pretty sure our next rendezvous will end up being our last.

"I'm, um, coming up with something good," I say half-heartedly. "Just give me a few more minutes."

"What's the story with that girl from the hospital?" Kid Supreme asks. "I thought she was joining us."

So did I. Unfortunately, Haywire didn't commit. While she agreed that Harmony sounded like a major threat, she wasn't sure she could handle leaving the hospital right now. So, I'm not sure if she'll be with us or not. But until I know, I don't want to rule her out.

"She'll be joining us, um, later," I say, trying to sound confident. "Dog-Gone is with her now. I'm just trying to figure out how best to—"

BEEP! BEEP! BEEP!

"What's that?" Kid Supreme asks.

"That's a transmission alert!" Grace says. "It could be the Freedom Force trying to reach us. Darn it! I knew I should have stayed by the computer. Quick, to the Mission Room!"

We sprint down the hall, and when we enter the Mission Room the monitor is flashing the words: RECEIVE TRANSMISSION?

"Move over," Grace says as she nudges past me to get to the console. Then, she looks at the monitor and says, "Hang on. This isn't coming from space." She hits a few buttons on the keyboard, and then, to my surprise, Harmony's face appears on the screen!

"Epic Zero, this message is for you," Harmony says.

Suddenly, my heart starts beating fast. I mean, how did she even know where to find me? Then, the camera pulls back and I realize she's standing inside an ancient-looking arena.

"Hey, that's the Colosseum," Kid Supreme says.

"You know, the Roman arena where they held gladiator fights."

Oh. Wonderful.

"Epic Zero, it is time to end this," Harmony says matter-of-factly. "You claim to be a brave hero, so I challenge you to show me how brave you truly are. I invite you to meet me here, at the Roman Colosseum, for one last showdown. I cannot think of a more fitting venue for our final encounter, for one of us will live and the other will die."

D-Die? I swallow hard.

"If you require additional motivation to face me here," she continues, "I will provide it for you now."

Suddenly, the camera pulls back farther and my jaw drops. Lying on a stone slab in front of Harmony is Selfie—and her arms and legs are tied to stakes! I can see that she's still breathing, but she's not moving.

"If you decline my challenge," Harmony continues, raising a silver dagger, "then I will be forced to sacrifice this girl you are so fond of." Then, she strokes Selfie's cheek and says, "It would be a shame to kill one so loyal, but alas, all is fair in love and war. So, Epic Zero, the choice is yours. Face me in battle or the blood of this girl will be on your hands. Oh, and if you are brave enough to come, then for her sake, I suggest you come alone." She smiles menacingly, and the transmission suddenly ends.

I-I can't believe it. While I've been up here trying to formulate a plan, Harmony beat me to the punch!

And she's using Selfie as bait!

"It's a trap," Kid Supreme says.

"Of course, it's a trap," Grace says, crossing her arms. "But the question is, what are we going to do about it? If Harmony is some sort of a Goddess then who knows what she's capable of? I don't even know if she can be killed. We can't just let him walk in there to face her alone."

"Sorry," I say, "but that's exactly what I have to do. You both heard her, she'll kill Selfie if I don't. Trap or no trap, Harmony knows I have to save Selfie. Nothing else matters."

"But she'll kill you!" Grace says.

"That's her plan," I say. "But listen up, because I've come up with a plan of my own."

***

I land the Gen-Jet in the center of Rome just outside of the Colosseum. I can see why it's one of the Seven Wonders of the World. It's a magnificent stadium, even as ruins, with its oval shape and arcade of arches.

On the way over, I learned that it was built in 80 AD. The structure is massive, standing twelve stories high and six hundred feet wide. In its day, it could hold fifty thousand spectators who would come to watch gladiator fights, animal hunts, and (gulp) public executions.

As I step out of the Gen-Jet, I feel like I've been

transported back in time. I can imagine hearing the roars of the lions and the cheers of the bloodthirsty crowds. Sadly, lots of innocent people died here. I just hope Selfie and I aren't next.

I glance up at the clear, blue sky. Grace and Kid Supreme are watching me from somewhere up high. They wanted to face Harmony with me but I wouldn't let them. After all, the last thing I need is to put Selfie's life in even more danger. So, they're up there waiting for me to say the secret words we agreed on. Until then, they're not to interfere, no matter how bad it looks.

It's eerily quiet as I walk through the entrance. Strangely, there's no one around, which I'm guessing is exactly how Harmony wants it. As I step onto the dirt floor of the arena, I'm walking in the footsteps of real gladiators. These days, however, the floor of the arena is missing in large areas, revealing a tunnel system used to lift fighters and animals through trap doors to do battle.

I look up at the remains of the terraces circling the arena. I read that your status determined where you sat, with the emperor and his senators closest to the action. Unfortunately, I won't be a spectator for today's games. Instead, I'm a participant, and my opponent is waiting for me on the other side of the arena.

"Welcome," Harmony says, "to your death."

I ignore her dramatic greeting and focus on Selfie, who is still knocked out. "Let her go!" I call out. I concentrate hard and try to copy Harmony's powers, whatever they are, but just like Suadela's eye, I don't sense any Meta energy to grab onto.

"I think not," Harmony says, holding her dagger over Selfie's chest. "Look around you. This arena was built for blood. Many mortal men, women, and children died in this arena to honor the Gods. I could not imagine a better place to end your life."

There she goes with that 'Gods' stuff again. Well, it's time I found out the truth. I need to know if my theory is correct. She baited me, now let's see if I can bait her.

"That was a long time ago," I say. "No one worships the Roman Gods anymore. They're old news."

"Unfortunately, you are correct," Harmony says with a frown. "But there was a time when the Gods were everything. Back then, mortals believed the Gods controlled every aspect of their measly lives… and they worshipped us. Every God and Goddess ruled over a specific domain, and the humans prayed to us, sacrificed for us, and showered us with gifts to win our favor. That was the Golden Age. The world was filled with worshippers and we were young and strong. Although we took tribute from mortals, we gave as much as we received. For in return for their loyalty, we provided aid, guidance, and protection."

I was right! The way she's talking, she's making it seem like she is some kind of a Goddess!

"But gradually things began to change," Harmony continues, her voice falling. "Over time, the mortals stopped worshipping us. The most insignificant among us, like Suadela, felt the impact first. Despite the importance of her domain, she was unable to build a strong following. As her limited number of worshippers waned, so did she. First, her power weakened, and then her physical form followed. Before long, she had transformed from a living, breathing Goddess to a mere statue of herself."

Holy cow! I was right about that too! Suadela was once alive! Which means that all of those other statues under the Pantheon were once alive too!

"I, however, was more fortunate than Suadela," Harmony says. "At first, my base of worshippers was large, but that too dwindled as time progressed. Yet, my domain remained relevant, even in the modern age. And while mortals no longer prayed to me or made sacrifices in my name in exchange for my good favor, they still desired the domain I ruled. They needed it, begged for it, even killed for it. And as a result, I managed to cling to my existence. I was weak, feeble, a shell of my former self—but I was alive. All the while, I never forgot what it was like to be worshipped—and I swore I would regain my power one day."

Her words send chills down my spine. There's no doubt about it, she's some sort of a Goddess. But who?

"So, I carefully observed the human race," Harmony continues. "I watched them for centuries, trying to find a way to regain the status I had lost. It seemed hopeless, until one day a new kind of mortal appeared. To my surprise, they had powers like the Gods. They could fly, or heal, or perform great feats of strength. They were called Metas."

M-Metas?

"Suddenly, my path became clear," she continues. "Regular mortals worshipped Metas, just like they used to worship the Gods of old. Of course, the mortals no longer made sacrifices, but they were obsessed with these superhuman beings. So, I studied countless Metas over the years. What made some popular and others obscure? Once I had my answer, I remade myself into the ultimate Meta—Harmony! Using this identity, I created a mission that appealed to the innermost desire of all mortals living in today's chaotic world—a desire for true and lasting peace. And it worked like a charm. The world flocked to support me, and the more followers I gained, the stronger I became."

"Wait a minute, so that's what this is all about?" I say. "You don't really care about world peace or ending hunger. You're doing this just to get people to worship you again. You're doing this so you can relive your glory days?!"

"Fool!" Harmony shouts. "How dare you question the motivations of a Goddess. My power, my beauty, is wholly dependent upon the adoration of your meager kind. I will not have it stolen away again by an insignificant ant like you!"

Her… beauty?

Suddenly, everything clicks.

But… that can't be possible, can it?

I have to know for sure.

"Um, earlier you said your domain is still relevant today," I say, swallowing hard. "So, if you don't mind me asking, exactly which domain is that?"

Harmony's lips curl into a menacing smile, and then she says, "Love."

Love?

As in, the Goddess of Love?

"Y-You're Venus?!" I blurt out.

"Very good," she says, raising her dagger over Selfie's heart. "And speaking of love, I know you care deeply for your friend here, so I will give you a choice. If you take her place on my altar, you can sacrifice your life in exchange for hers. You can decide who lives and who dies in the name of love."

Meta Profile

Kid Supreme

Name: Carlos Ruiz	Height: 5'10"
Race: Human	Weight: 195 lbs
Status: Hero/Active	Eyes/Hair: Brown/Black

META 3: Multi-Meta Powers
Extreme Invulnerability
Can Only Use One of These Extreme Powers at a Time: Strength, Speed, Heat Vision, Enhanced Senses, or Flight

Observed Characteristics	
Combat 95	
Durability 100	Leadership 53
Strategy 74	Willpower 95

FIFTEEN

I HATE LOVE

This is insane.

Not only is Harmony actually Venus—you know, the Roman Goddess of Love—but now she's offering me the choice to save Selfie's life by taking her place as a sacrifice! Of course, under normal circumstances, I wouldn't volunteer to be hogtied and skewered on an altar, but these aren't exactly normal circumstances. Venus knows I would do anything to save Selfie, which leaves me with only one option.

"Okay, I'll do it," I say without hesitation. "Just lower the knife and let her go."

"Excellent," Harmony—or rather, Venus—says with an evil smile. Then, she unties Selfie and lifts her limp body off the altar with ease. Unfortunately, Venus is holding the dagger up to Selfie's neck.

I swallow hard. Well, this wasn't in the plan, but at least it gets me closer to Selfie. Hopefully, I can ensure her safety before Venus kills me.

"Come, child," Venus says. "Come take her place."

We're standing on opposite sides of the Colosseum, so I have to cross the exposed arena floor to get to them. I climb over the railing and drop down onto one of the tunnel walls. Then, I do my best tightrope walker impression as I carefully make my way to the other side. Once I'm there, I climb over the railing and onto their platform.

"Okay, I'm here," I say, bending over to catch my breath. "Now give me Selfie."

"Oh, I think not," Venus says, throwing Selfie over her shoulder like a sack of potatoes. "Lie on my altar. I will release your friend after you are secured."

I hesitate. I mean, can I really trust her to let Selfie go? "How do I know you'll stick to your word?" I ask.

"As Harmony, you have seen me do everything I had promised," she says. "Is that not enough? Now, do not delay. I bore easily." Then, she presses the flat part of the blade against Selfie's neck.

I don't feel good about it, but there's nothing I can do. She did deliver on her promises as Harmony, so I can only hope that she'll do the same now. I climb up onto the cold, stone altar.

"Lie flat on your back," Venus says.

"There," I say, lying down. "Now it's your turn."

"After you are secured, remember?" she says.

Suddenly, the ropes take on a life of their own! They wrap tightly around my limbs and pull themselves taut.

Ouch! That hurts!

"Now, I will fulfill my end of the bargain," she says. Then, she SNAPS her fingers, and Selfie vanishes!

"Selfie!" I call out, straining against the ropes. "What did you do to her?"

"Do not despair," Venus says. "She is safe with my other devotees. I am glad I did not have to dispose of her. She is useful and her loyal worship adds to my strength."

Well, now that Selfie is out of this mess, phase one of my plan is complete. Of course, I didn't expect to be in this vulnerable position, but I need to keep moving forward. Time to distract Venus for phase two.

That is, if there even is a phase two.

"Now, we shall commence with the sacrifice," Venus says, moving toward me.

"Um, can we talk about that?" I ask. "I mean, I've got nothing against love. I used to give Valentine's Day cards to every kid in my elementary school. Of course, I never received any cards back, but—"

"Silence!" she yells, raising the dagger over her head.

This is it! I hope this works. Please, please work.

Suddenly, I hear PANTING. Yes!

"Dog-Gone, now!" I yell.

I turn my head to see Dog-Gone and Haywire appear out of thin air—right behind Venus!

I can't believe it! Haywire came!

"Die, mortal!" Venus shouts as she thrusts the dagger down at my chest!

No! We're too late!

I close my eyes and brace myself for pain, when—

CLUNK!

Venus' dagger presses down hard against my chest, knocking the wind out of me, but… it doesn't feel like I've been stabbed. I look down, expecting to see Venus' knife sticking out of me, but instead, the eye amulet is sitting on top of my 'no' insignia, and Venus' dagger is protruding from the center of Suadela's eye!

"N-NO!" Venus shouts in dismay as she pulls her dagger out of Suadela's now-damaged eye.

Yes! It worked! My plan actually worked!

I wasn't sure if Haywire's bad luck power would work on Harmony/Venus, but I was pretty sure it would work wonders on the simple chain holding the eye amulet around her neck! And just as I hoped, Haywire's powers made Venus' amulet unclasp and fall onto my chest right before she stabbed me! So Venus plunged her dagger into her own amulet instead of me!

"The eye…" Venus says, her own eyes widening in disbelief. "What… what did you do?"

"You told me that only a God could destroy another God, right?" I say. "So, I made sure that you destroyed Suadela's eye with your own hand. Now you've lost the power to persuade anyone to do anything. Not bad for a mere mortal, huh?"

"I-I will kill you," Venus says, turning to face Dog-Gone and Haywire. "I will kill you all!"

As I see the fear growing in Haywire's eyes, I remember I promised her that she wouldn't have to fight!

"Dog-Gone!" I yell. "Get Haywire and get invisible!"

Dog-Gone gums Haywire's wrist and they disappear.

"Come back!" Venus yells. Then, she frantically starts touching her face and howls, "Nooooo!"

Suddenly, Venus' appearance changes right before my eyes—she grows several inches in height, her blond hair turns scraggly white, and her perfectly smooth skin becomes all wrinkly! I-I can't believe it. She's an ancient woman!

And that's when I realize what just happened. Venus wasn't only using Suadela's eye to get everyone to worship her, she was also using it to make us think she looked like a young, vibrant girl! But now that the eye is destroyed, the real Venus has been revealed!

"M—My beauty…" she says, feeling her haggard face. Then, she looks down at me enraged, and screams, "You! You will pay for this!"

Uh-oh. I pull hard against the ropes but they're not giving! I've got to get out of here! Then, I remember there was a third phase to my plan. My secret words to call for backup!

"JELLY DOUGHNU—"

Suddenly, there's an orange blur, and—POW!

Kid Supreme socks Venus, who goes flying across the Colosseum. Then, Grace lands and unties my feet.

"Thanks!" I say.

"You sure waited long enough," Grace says as she frees my wrists. "Kid Supreme was listening with his Super Hearing, but I was worried that you forgot what the secret words were."

"Sorry," I say. "I had to make sure that Venus destroyed the amulet first."

"So, that's Venus huh?" Grace says. "I thought she was supposed to be drop-dead gorgeous."

"Well, she nailed the drop-dead part," I say, sliding off the altar.

"Mortal scum!" Venus screams, pointing at me as she gets back to her feet. "You ruined everything! You destroyed centuries of planning! Now you will know the full wrath of a Goddess!"

Suddenly, Venus' body glows with a strange, blue energy. Then, she raises her arms and transforms into a gigantic, white bird that's bigger than a delivery truck!

"Whoa! What is that?" Grace asks.

"It's a dove," Kid Supreme says. "In ancient mythology, Venus was associated with doves which are symbols of purity, love, and peace."

"Die!" comes Venus' voice out of the dove's beak.

"I don't think this dove is interested in peace," I say. "Look out!"

Venus flaps her massive wings and charges at us.

"I'll handle this," Kid Supreme says confidently as he steps in front of us.

He rears back his fist, but Venus is coming so—

THOOM!

Grace pulls me behind the altar as Kid Supreme's body CRASHES through the wall behind us! Then, Venus lands on top of the altar and looks down at us with her big, beady, bird eyes.

"Move!" I shout, pushing Grace out of the way as Venus PECKS through the floor between us!

"Get out of here!" I yell to Grace.

"I'd love to," Grace says, taking to the air, "but Mom and Dad would take my phone for a week if I let you croak."

Gee, I can feel the sisterly love.

"Yo, bird brain!" Grace shouts as she circles around Venus. "Come and get me!"

"Are you nuts?" I yell. "What are you doing?"

"Distracting her," Grace says as Venus swats at her with an enormous wing. "Now do something!"

I'd love to but what can I do? Then, it hits me. I can't use my powers on Venus, but I can use them on someone else. I concentrate hard but don't sense Haywire anywhere in the vicinity, which means Dog-Gone actually did his job for once. So, I go for the next best option.

As Kid Supreme climbs out of the hole in the wall, I bathe him with my powers and pull it back. As his Meta energy flows through me, I get that strange, familiar sensation all over again. But this time I realize where I've experienced that feeling before and my stomach sinks.

Meta-Man.

I can't believe I didn't make the connection earlier. Meta-Man had Flight, Heat-Vision, Super-Speed, Super-Strength, and more, and so does Kid Supreme! Meta-Man could only use one power at a time and, come to think of it, I don't think I've seen Kid Supreme use more than one power at a time either. Kid Supreme is an all-powerful superhero. Meta-Man was an all-powerful superhero too.

That is, until he wasn't.

"Yo!" Grace yells. "Are you gonna help me or what?"

Grace! Venus is chasing her in the air. I raise my fist to take flight but nothing happens. Ugh! At the Pantheon, I knew Kid Supreme was using his Flight power, but now I have no clue what I've got.

"Help!" Grace shouts.

Instinct takes over, and my eyes narrow as Venus flies overhead. The next thing I know—FAZOOM—red lasers shoot out of my eyes and strike Venus squarely on her left wing. It's a direct hit!

Suddenly, Venus spirals down with a trail of smoke and CRASHES into the center of the Colosseum!

Wow! That's the first time I've ever used Heat Vision and it's freaking awesome!

"About time," Grace says, landing beside me.

But my smile is quickly wiped from my face as we

hear RUMBLING followed by a BOOM! I shield my body as debris explodes everywhere, and when I look back up, Venus has emerged from the rubble. She's back in Goddess form, and even though her left arm is smoking, she's moving it around just fine!

"You caught me by surprise," she says. "But your time in this world ends now."

"I don't think so, lady," Kid Supreme says as he lands in front of her.

"You are strong," she says to him. "But you are no God."

Then, she PUNCHES him in the face, but he doesn't even flinch.

"What?" she says, looking curiously at her fist. "My power. It's… weakening."

"Well, you might be a God," Kid Supreme says, "but you're God-awful ugly!"

Then, he SLUGS her so hard she goes flying into a wall! Suddenly, I hear the sound of an ENGINE overhead, and when I look up I see the Game Changers' jet coming in for a landing!

"Get ready," I say to Grace. "Because here come Venus' minions."

As the jet touches down, the doors open and all of the Game Changers come leaping out, including Pinball, Night Owl, Skunk Girl… and Selfie! I'm so happy to see she's okay! But then my heart sinks when she joins the others behind Venus.

"Your timing is perfect, my loyal followers," Venus says to the Game Changers as she gets back on her feet. "Do not be alarmed. My appearance may have changed but I am still Harmony. Though, you can now call me by my true name, Venus. These worthless insects are standing in the way of our progress. I command you to kill them. Kill them all!"

Oh boy, here we go again.

"Your wish is our command," Supersize says, growing a hundred feet tall. "One crushed insect coming up." Then, she raises her fist and SLAMS it down on top of Venus!

What? But then I remember that Venus' amulet is destroyed! Which means that she's lost her influence over everyone!

"Idiots!" Venus says as she slowly pulls herself out of the giant crater Supersize pounded her into. "Y-You worship me! I am your leader!"

"Not anymore," Thermo says. "We've come to our senses and we don't follow creeps like you!"

"That's right!" Selfie says. "Next Gen, attack!"

Wait, did she just say, 'Next Gen?'

"Need a lift?" Night Owl asks, wrapping Venus in a shadow and throwing her high into the air.

"Cowabunga!" Pinball cries as he SLAMS into Venus, knocking her to the ground again.

"Here's a smell as rotten as you are," Skunk Girl says, drenching Venus in green stink.

I-I can't believe it. My team is back!

"E-Enough," Venus says as she staggers to her feet, fanning Skunk Girl's odor away. "M-My strength is weakening," she mutters. Then, she looks straight into my eyes and says, "This is far from over, mortal. I will get my revenge one day soon."

She raises her arms and her body starts glowing with that weird, blue energy.

"She's transforming again!" Grace shouts.

Before I can react, Venus changes into a giant, white dove and lifts into the air! But as she flaps her wings, she barely gets off the ground. Suddenly, her shape starts glitching in the air, alternating between a dove and her normal self!

"Look out!" Kid Supreme shouts as Venus' form transforms back to herself and drops from the sky like a lead ball, landing hard on the platform a few steps away from me!

She's on her hands and knees, breathing hard. I guess that without any worshippers, her powers are fading fast! In fact, she's so weak her entire body is… shaking?

"Y-You did this," she labors to say as she looks at me with steely eyes, "I… will… KILL YOU!"

Suddenly, she pulls her dagger from the folds of her robe and lunges at me!

"Epic!" Selfie calls out.

Venus' outstretched hand reaches for my neck while her other hand hoists the dagger high in the air!

I stagger backward but it's too late!

As she begins to thrust down, I close my eyes, and brace myself for—

CRAAAACCCCCKKKKKLLLLLEEEEE!

Huh? What was that? I open my eyes and Venus is still in front of me holding the knife over her head, but she's turned into a… a… statue?!

"Are you okay, Epic?" Selfie asks as she runs over and hugs me.

"Maybe?" I answer as I stare at the statue of Venus in shock.

"Dude, I thought you were a goner," Kid Supreme says, feeling Venus' solid, marble arm. "Now she's like all the Gods beneath the Pantheon."

I breathe in deeply and exhale. She almost had me, but I got lucky the sudden lack of worshippers caught up with her.

"Epic, are you sure you're okay?" Selfie asks, putting her hand on my shoulder.

"Yeah," I say, ignoring Grace's smirk. "How about you? Are you okay?"

"I'm fine," she says. "But everything is so foggy I don't know what happened. The last thing I remember is meeting up with Harmony while you and Kid Supreme were off on a mission. The next thing I know, I'm sitting inside the Game Changers' jet."

"Wait, so are you saying you didn't join the Game Changers voluntarily?" I ask.

"The Game Changers?" Selfie says. "Why would I do that?"

"Oh, it's a long story," I say as relief floods over me.

"I'm glad we were hovering close by," Thermo says. "We didn't know what was happening at first, but then we saw all of the commotion here at the Colosseum and came to help."

"Yeah," Supersize says. "I guess Venus wanted us nearby in case she ran into trouble."

"Well, she won't be running anywhere any time soon," Skunk Girl says, knocking on Venus' solid back.

"So, what now?" Grace asks.

"Now?" I say, looking at Venus. "Now we need to find a home for this statue. A very, very safe home."

Meta Profile

Venus

▯ Name: Venus	▯ Height: 6’0”
▯ Race: Olympian	▯ Weight: Unknown
▯ Status: Goddess of Love	▯ Eyes/Hair: Blue/White

Meta Power: Incalculable
▯ Power and vitality dependent on number of worshippers
▯ Possesses incredible strength and durability at full power
▯ Can transform into a dove

Observed Characteristics	
Combat +++	
Durability +++	Leadership +++
Strategy +++	Willpower +++

EPILOGUE

I MAKE SEVERAL ANNOUNCEMENTS

I can hardly contain my excitement.

The Freedom Force finally returned from their off-world mission, and after a few days of rest we've all gathered in the Trophy Room at the Beacon for a special announcement. As I look at the smiling faces in front of me it feels like a dream. I mean, it's amazing to have everyone together again.

"So, are you going to get on with it or what?" Grace barks, crossing her arms. "I've got a million places I'd rather be right now."

Well, almost everyone.

"Patience, Glory Girl," Dad says. "This is a special moment for Next Gen. There's no need to rush."

"Why thank you, Captain Justice," I say smugly.

My heart swells with joy as I look at my team. I'm so

happy to be with them again after I almost lost them. This time we're sticking together! Next Gen is back!

But that's not all that's back! After we destroyed the eye of Suadela and stopped Venus, the world returned to normal. Well, 'normal' is a relative term because nations have defaulted back to their old ways of doing business, including rebuilding weapons, hoarding resources, and overlooking the less fortunate. That's not good, but this time I plan to bring some change of my own.

And speaking of change, I was surprised the Game Changers decided to stick together after the truth came out. According to Thermo, they didn't remember being a team, but they decided to give it a try without being under the influence of Venus. I wished them the best of luck and offered our support if they needed it. I suspect we'll be seeing them again, hopefully under better circumstances.

"Epic Zero? Are you ready for the big reveal?" Mom asks, snapping me back to reality.

"Oh, yes we are," I say quickly, taking hold of the cloth covering the display case. "First, we would like to thank you all again for giving us this amazing headquarters. Especially you, TechnocRat."

"Aw, shucks," TechnocRat says, touching his little heart. "I'm just hoping there's Camembert cheese under that cloth."

"Unfortunately, no," I say. "But we do have something pretty special. We've asked you to join us today as we unveil the first trophy in our fantastic, new Trophy Room. Now, before the big reveal, I'll recap the harrowing events that led to this wonderful—"

"Are you serious?" Grace blurts out. "Get to the stinking trophy already!"

"Okay, okay," I say annoyed. Well, so much for the pomp and circumstance. "Ladies and gentlemen, here it is! The eye of Suadela!"

Then, I whip off the cloth, revealing the eye amulet sitting on a stand inside the display case. Of course, it's damaged and useless thanks to Venus, but I think that makes it extra special. It's a real battle souvenir.

Everyone applauds.

"Congratulations," Shadow Hawk says.

"Well earned," Blue Bolt adds.

For a brief second, I considered adding the statue of Venus to our trophy collection, but it just seemed too dangerous. I mean, what if she changed back? So instead, we turned her over to TechnocRat who built a super-secure containment cell for her on Lockdown, which is still going strong by the way.

"Thank you," I say. "It was truly a team effort. Of course, there is one person in particular we would like to thank. And that's—"

Kid Supreme flashes a big smile and steps forward.

"—Haywire," I finish.

Kid Supreme steps back sheepishly as everyone applauds around him.

"None of this would have been possible without Haywire," I continue. "Her bravery and willingness to help were truly inspiring."

After everything settled down, I visited her in the hospital to thank her, but surprisingly she thanked me instead. She said that I inspired her to work harder to control her powers so she could live a normal life. I was so happy for her. Then, I said goodbye and faceplanted into the door.

Gotta love Haywire.

As I look at Suadela's eye, I wonder what happened to the other statues beneath the Pantheon. I was worried someone might find them and use them for evil, just like Venus did with Suadela's eye. But when we returned to the Pantheon to collect them they were gone. I don't know what happened to them, and I don't have a good feeling about it either.

"That was very touching," Grace says. "Can I split now?"

"Hold on," Selfie says. "There's more. Right, Epic?"

"More?" I ask as she gives me a death glare.

"Oh, right, more," I say. Honestly, I was kind of hoping she'd forget but I guess she didn't. "Well—ahem—we would also like to, um, recognize someone else who, uh, bravely fought by our side. And to recognize his accomplishments, the team, well, most of the team anyway, has decided to, um, er, officially, uh…"

"Epic!" Selfie whispers sternly.

"Fine," I say, my shoulders sagging. "We'd like to officially invite Kid Supreme to join the team."

"What?" Kid Supreme says. "Really? You're ending my trial period early?"

"Well, I mean, we don't have to if you don't want us to," I say, pepping up. "You can stay on a trial period if you really—"

"No, I'd be honored to join you," Kid Supreme says.

"Yes!" Skunk Girl says, pumping her fist.

"Thanks!" Kid Supreme says, giving me a firm handshake that leaves my hand throbbing.

What can I do? I was essentially outvoted. I told the team what I discovered about Kid Supreme's powers but they weren't concerned about it. According to Selfie, he's not Meta-Man and he's proven himself to be an asset to the team. I may have lost the vote but I can assure you of one thing, I'll be keeping a close eye on him.

"Okay, so that's done. See ya suckers," Grace says, turning for the exit.

"Hold it," I say. "I have one more announcement."

"You've got to be kidding me," she says, stopping in her tracks.

"No," I say. "Listen, even though Harmony turned out to be an evil Goddess, she wasn't all wrong. I mean, we're Metas, right? We can do more than just fight bad guys. So, I've arranged for us to collect excess food and deliver it to people in need around the world. And we're scheduled to leave right now."

"Epic, seriously?" Selfie says. "That's amazing!"

"What a great idea," Mom says.

"Okay, that was worth sticking around for," Grace says, punching me in the arm.

"We'll warm up the Gen-Jet," Night Owl says. "Come on, Next Gen."

"I guess that includes me," Kid Supreme says.

As my friends pile into the cargo elevator and head for the Hangar, Dad puts his arm around me and says, "You know, I could learn a thing or two about leadership from you."

"Really?" I say. "Gee, thanks."

"<SQUAWK> Epic?" comes Selfie's voice over the intercom. "Epic, are you there?"

I run over to the wall panel and push the intercom button. "Yeah, what's up?"

"Pinball is stuck in the elevator doors again," she says. "Can you get him out?"

"AVA, really?" I say. "Okay, I'll be right there." Then, I turn to TechnocRat and say, "Hey, 'Mighty and Brilliant' TechnocRat, boy do I have a to-do list for you."

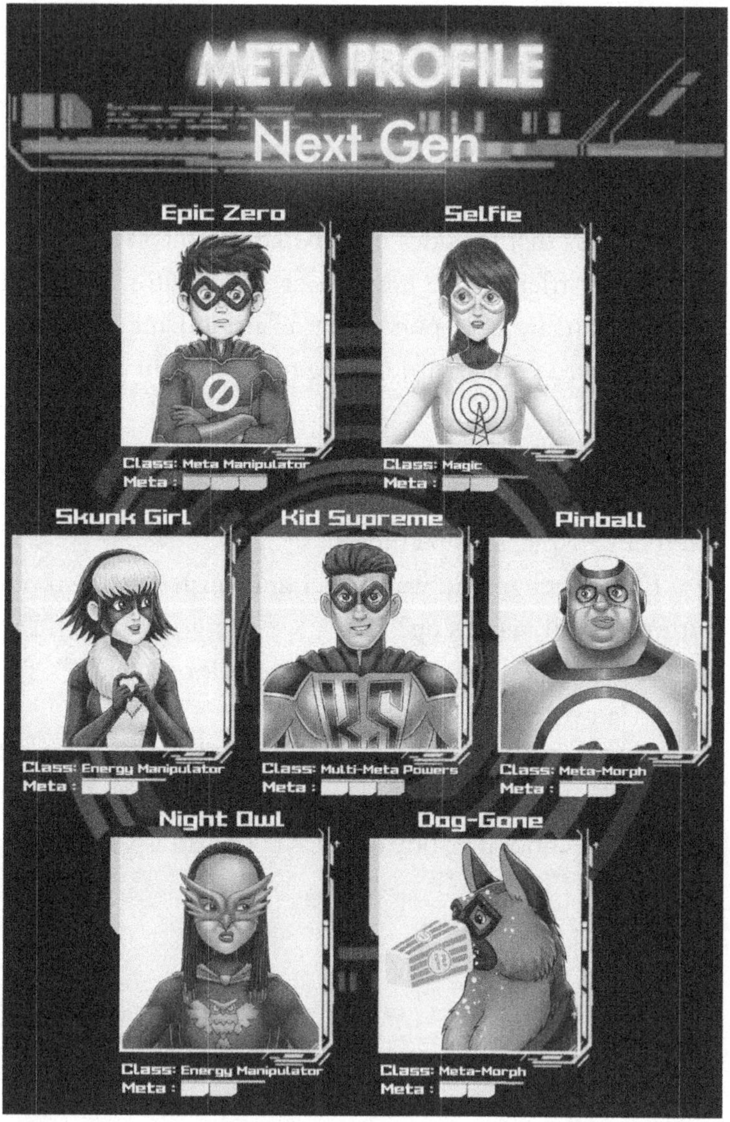
META PROFILE
Next Gen
Epic Zero
Class: Meta Manipulator
Meta :
Selfie
Class: Magic
Meta :
Skunk Girl
Class: Energy Manipulator
Meta :
Kid Supreme
Class: Multi-Meta Powers
Meta :
Pinball
Class: Meta-Morph
Meta :
Night Owl
Class: Energy Manipulator
Meta :
Dog-Gone
Class: Meta-Morph
Meta :

EPIC ZERO 11 IS AVAILABLE NOW!

Mars, the God of War, is attempting to start World War III! To stop him, Minerva, the Goddess of Wisdom, has presented Elliott, Kid Supreme, and Pinball with a quest. They must bring her the three Weapons of Power so she can stop Mars. But Mars has sent his own champions to retrieve the powerful artifacts, and whoever gets them first will determine the fate of the world!

Get EPIC ZERO 11:
Tales of a Mere Meta Mortal today!

YOU CAN MAKE A BIG DIFFERENCE

Calling all heroes! I need your help to get Epic Zero 10 in front of more readers.

Reviews are extremely helpful in getting attention for my books. I wish I had the marketing muscle of the major publishers, but instead, I have something far more valuable, loyal readers, just like you! Your generosity in providing an honest review will help bring this book to the attention of more readers.

So, if you enjoyed this book, I would be very grateful if you could spare a minute to leave a review on the book's Amazon page. Thanks for your support!

Stay Epic!

R.L. Ullman

META POWERS GLOSSARY

FROM THE META MONITOR:

There are nine known Meta power classifications. These classifications have been established to simplify Meta identification and provide a quick framework to understand a Meta's potential powers and capabilities. **Note:** Metas can possess powers in more than one classification. In addition, Metas can evolve over time in both the powers they express, as well as the effectiveness of their powers.

Due to the wide range of Meta abilities, superpowers have been further segmented into power levels. Power levels differ across Meta power classifications. In general, the following power levels have been established:

- Meta 0: Displays no Meta power.
- Meta 1: Displays limited Meta power.
- Meta 2: Displays considerable Meta power.
- Meta 3: Displays extreme Meta power.

The following is a brief overview of the nine Meta power classifications.

ENERGY MANIPULATION:

Energy Manipulation is the ability to generate, shape, or act as a conduit for various forms of energy. Energy Manipulators can control energy by focusing or redirecting energy toward a specific target or shaping/reshaping energy for a specific task. Energy Manipulators are often impervious to the forms of energy they can manipulate.

Examples of the types of energies utilized by Energy Manipulators include, but are not limited to:

- Atomic
- Chemical
- Cosmic
- Electricity
- Gravity
- Heat
- Light
- Magnetic
- Sound
- Space
- Time

Note: the fundamental difference between an Energy Manipulator and a Meta-morph with Energy Manipulation capability is that an Energy Manipulator does not change their physical, molecular state to either generate or transfer energy (see META-MORPH).

FLIGHT:
Flight is the ability to fly, glide, or levitate above the Earth's surface without the use of an external source (e.g. jetpack). Flight can be accomplished through a variety of methods, these include, but are not limited to:

- Reversing the forces of gravity
- Riding air currents
- Using planetary magnetic fields
- Wings

Metas exhibiting Flight can range from barely sustaining flight a few feet off the ground to reaching the far limits of outer space.

Often, Metas with Flight ability also display the complementary ability of Super-Speed. However, it can be difficult to decipher if Super-Speed is a Meta power in its own right or is simply a function of combining the Meta's Flight ability with the Earth's natural gravitational force.

MAGIC:
Magic is the ability to display a wide variety of Meta abilities by channeling the powers of a secondary magical or mystical source. Known secondary sources of Magic powers include, but are not limited to:

- Alien lifeforms
- Dark arts
- Demonic forces
- Departed souls
- Mystical spirits

Typically, the forces of Magic are channeled through an enchanted object. Known magical, enchanted objects include:

- Amulets
- Books
- Cloaks
- Gemstones
- Wands

- Weapons

Some Magicians can transport themselves into the mystical realm of their magical source. They may also have the ability to transport others into and out of these realms as well.

Note: the fundamental difference between a Magician and an Energy Manipulator is that a Magician typically channels their powers from a mystical source that likely requires the use of an enchanted object to express these powers (see ENERGY MANIPULATOR).

META MANIPULATION:
Meta Manipulation is the ability to duplicate or negate the Meta powers of others. Meta Manipulation is a rare Meta power and can be extremely dangerous if the Meta Manipulator is capable of manipulating the powers of multiple Metas at one time. Meta Manipulators who can manipulate the powers of several Metas at once have been observed to reach Meta 4 power levels.

Based on the unique powers of the Meta Manipulator, it is hypothesized that other abilities could include altering or controlling the powers of others. Despite their tremendous abilities, Meta Manipulators are often unable to generate powers of their own and are limited to manipulating the powers of others. When not utilizing their abilities, Meta Manipulators may be vulnerable to attack.

Note: It has been observed that a Meta Manipulator requires close physical proximity to a Meta target to fully manipulate their power. When fighting a Meta

Manipulator, it is advised to stay at a reasonable distance and to attack from long range. Meta Manipulators have been observed manipulating the powers of others up to one hundred yards away.

META-MORPH:

Meta-morph is the ability to display a wide variety of Meta abilities by "morphing" all, or part, of one's physical form from one state into another. There are two sub-types of Meta-morphs:

- Physical
- Molecular

Physical morphing occurs when a Meta-morph transforms their physical state to express their powers. Physical Meta-morphs typically maintain their human physiology while exhibiting their powers (with the exception of Shapeshifters). Types of Physical morphing include, but are not limited to:

- Invisibility
- Malleability (elasticity/plasticity)
- Physical by-products (silk, toxins, etc…)
- Shapeshifting
- Size changes (larger or smaller)

Molecular morphing occurs when a Meta-morph transforms their molecular state from a normal physical state to a non-physical state to express their powers. Types of Molecular morphing include, but are not limited to:

- Fire
- Ice
- Rock
- Sand
- Steel
- Water

Note: Because Meta-morphs can display abilities that mimic all other Meta power classifications, it can be difficult to properly identify a Meta-morph upon the first encounter. However, it is critical to carefully observe how their powers manifest, and, if it is through Physical or Molecular morphing, you can be certain you are dealing with a Meta-morph.

PSYCHIC:

Psychic is the ability to use one's mind as a weapon. There are two sub-types of Psychics:

- Telepaths
- Telekinetics

Telepathy is the ability to read and influence the thoughts of others. While Telepaths often do not appear to be physically intimidating, their power to penetrate minds can often result in more devastating damage than a physical assault.

Telekinesis is the ability to manipulate physical objects with one's mind. Telekinetics can often move objects with their mind that are much heavier than they could move physically. Many Telekinetics can also make objects move at very high speeds.

Note: Psychics are known to strike from long distances, and, in a fight, it is advised to incapacitate them as quickly as possible. Psychics often become physically drained from the extended use of their powers.

SUPER-INTELLIGENCE:
Super-Intelligence is the ability to display levels of intelligence above standard genius intellect. Super-Intelligence can manifest in many forms, including, but not limited to:

- Superior analytical ability
- Superior information synthesizing
- Superior learning capacity
- Superior reasoning skills

Note: Super-Intellects continuously push the envelope in the fields of technology, engineering, and weapons development. Super-Intellects are known to invent new approaches to accomplish previously impossible tasks. When dealing with a Super-Intellect, you should be mentally prepared to face challenges that have never been encountered before. In addition, Super-Intellects can come in all shapes and sizes. The most advanced Super-Intellects have originated from non-human creatures.

SUPER-SPEED:
Super-Speed is the ability to display movement at remarkable physical speeds above standard levels of speed. Metas with Super-Speed often exhibit complementary abilities to movement that include, but are not limited to:

- Enhanced endurance
- Phasing through solid objects
- Super-fast reflexes
- Time travel

Note: Metas with Super-Speed often have an equally super metabolism, burning thousands of calories per minute, and requiring them to eat many extra meals a day to maintain consistent energy levels. It has been observed that Metas exhibiting Super-Speed are quick thinkers, making it difficult to keep up with their thought processes.

SUPER-STRENGTH:
Super-Strength is the ability to utilize muscles to display remarkable levels of physical strength above expected levels of strength. Metas with Super-Strength can lift or push objects that are well beyond the capability of an average member of their species. Metas exhibiting Super-Strength can range from lifting objects twice their weight to incalculable levels of strength allowing for the movement of planets.

Metas with Super-Strength often exhibit complementary abilities to strength that include, but are not limited to:

- Earthquake generation through stomping
- Enhanced jumping
- Invulnerability
- Shockwave generation through clapping

Note: Metas with Super-Strength may not always possess this strength evenly. Metas with Super-Strength have been observed to demonstrate powers in only one arm or leg.

META PROFILE CHARACTERISTICS

FROM THE META MONITOR:

In addition to having a strong working knowledge of a Meta's powers and capabilities, it is also imperative to understand the key characteristics that form the core of their character. When facing or teaming up with Metas, understanding their key characteristics will help you gain deeper insight into their mentality and strategic potential.

What follows is a brief explanation of the five key characteristics you should become familiar with. **Note**: the data that appears in each Meta profile has been compiled from live field activity.

COMBAT:

The ability to defeat a foe in hand-to-hand combat.

DURABILITY:

The ability to withstand significant wear, pressure, or damage.

LEADERSHIP:

The ability to lead a team of disparate personalities and powers to victory.

STRATEGY:

The ability to find, and successfully exploit, a foe's weakness.

WILLPOWER:

The ability to persevere, despite seemingly insurmountable odds.

Get the EPIC ZERO CHARACTER GUIDE at rlullman.com!

OTHER SERIES BY R.L. ULLMAN

UNLEGENDARY DRAGON SERIES

MONSTER PROBLEMS SERIES

ABOUT THE AUTHOR

R.L. Ullman is the bestselling, award-winning author of books for young readers, including the EPIC ZERO® series, the UNLEGENDARY DRAGON™ series, the MONSTER PROBLEMS series, and the PETUNIA THE UNICORN™ series. He writes the kinds of books he loved reading as a kid, featuring fast-paced action, laugh-out-loud humor, and lots of heart. R.L. lives in Connecticut with his laptop and family. Visit rlullman.com for signed books, special editions, book merchandise, and more!

CONNECT WITH R.L.

Join R.L.'s mailing list at rlullman.com for discounts, exclusive offers, free content, and notifications about new releases! See what R.L. is working on at r.l.ullman_author on Instagram and @authorRLUllman on Facebook.

ACKNOWLEDGMENTS

I couldn't have written these books without the support of my own team of Meta heroes. I would like to thank my wife, Lynn (a.k.a. Mrs. Marvelous); my son Matthew (a.k.a. Captain Creativity); and my daughter Olivia (a.k.a. Ms. Positivity). I would also like to thank all of the readers who have connected with Elliott and his epic universe!

Made in United States
North Haven, CT
23 July 2023

39404656R00114